So's Your Old Man

By
Jack Tomlinson

Bookman LLC
Publishing & Marketing

Providing Quality, Professional
Author Services

www.bookmanmarketing.com

ISBN: 1-59453-609-0

For Jake

Ships Happen.

CHAPTER 1

"Why or when things get started is about as predictable as why or when things will end." So says my notorious father. He has always operated on a different level and I told myself early on that the only thing for me to do was to contemplate his antics and try not to get sucked in. But inevitably I did and I still am.

His take of how he and mom got started and what evolved came in the customary elaborate package. I was hooked on Dad's stories, this was a favorite, so I occasionally asked and he would readily repeat the yarn. The details changed from version to version but I memorized the story the way I want it to be and I'll tell it to get this started.

The washed out, or possibly washed up blonde, had the aisle seat. She was curled up in an odd way with her feet up and her head down. Somehow the seat belt was fastened around her. The Bracs were not particularly large people, but they unconsciously took up a lot of space. Codfish Brac was no exception and he got tangled in the girl's clothing as he tried to ease past her and into his seat.

"Do you mind," she said and laid on a withering stare. The belt buckle on his genuine African safari jacket had dropped down the front of the young woman's blouse. As Codfish moved so did the flimsy top. Things sort of popped into view.

"Jesus Christ in spades, Madam, I'm sorry and embarrassed." He had an infectious smile and he used it as he reached to retrieve the wandering belt.

She slapped his hand and loudly said, "I'll do it, thank you. Just get away!" She fished, caught the buckle and handed it to him and he slid into the window seat.

TWA Flight 99 was headed to San Francisco from Washington, D.C. During that night 1954 would become 1955. The gala flight on New Year's Eve was the airline's effort to mark the occasion for some forty travelers. The service was amiable and festive and dinner included rare roast beef accompanied by liberal slugs of whatever one wanted to drink. Despite rules and regulations, the cabin crew had a nip or two of New Year's cheer as the little party floated along in calm skies. It was forced comraderie but pleasant enough for most. Second thoughts, if any, would come after the flight.

Codfish congratulated himself on the fortuitous seating arrangement and then took his time as he planned his strategy for boy meets girl. She was feigning sleep, he guessed. The blonde had turned so that she faced away from him and toward the aisle. It would be a tough maneuver to get a look at her face. However, the young man was resourceful as well as rude. He gave her an elbow to the knee which was just hard enough to make her jump. She turned, eyes wide open, and mouth working. "Hey, what the hell are you doing? You just hit me, you jerk. You're out of here. If you don't move I'm going to see to it that your ass gets put in a major sling." She sounded as she looked, which was quite pissed off.

Her seat-mate had mannerisms which even some actors never quite master. Codfish could control his expression while his quick tongue eased him around or through almost any situation. He put on his shamed-boy face. The large blue eyes were downcast with a peek upward at her every few seconds. "Look, I'm really terribly sorry. Believe me, that was an accident. I was just trying to position myself to get up without disturbing you. I thought we could, I mean, I thought I would join the party. What else can I say? If you want me to move, I most certainly will. This is the most embarrassing thing I've done in hours."

His eyes shifted; he appeared somewhat contrite. The girl took a moment to check him out. Despite his bullshit, she was sort of curious. The young man had slightly curly blond hair to go with his great blue eyes. The face was round but not full. You would expect fair skin to go with the other features, but that was not the case. Maybe he'd been out in the sun. Anyway, he looked interesting and he was not too big. Big often meant brutal or stupid or both.

Codfish pulled a few things out of the seat pocket and feigned a move to decamp. But he wasn't going anywhere.

The girl decided to give him a try. "Are you always this clumsy?"

He picked up a trace of a smile. Codfish cautioned himself; at this point one had to be extremely careful.

He had the first little opening. Screw it up and he would have to punt.

"Clumsy runs in my family." He nodded as if he agreed with himself. "I should introduce myself. My name is Codfish Brac." He offered his hand and a sincere expression.

"Did you say 'Codfish'?" She wore a suspicious look and barely touched his fingers.

"Well, that's sort of a nickname; my birth certificate reads W.T. Brac."

"W.T. The two initials?"

"That's it. Naming was always a problem in my family, so my ancestors moved to initials. It's a lot easier, and there are fewer fights."

"So, if I get this right, your family has spawned generations of initial-named people." She rolled her eyes.

"Yup, there are four of us initialed by my parents. Then I have a number of uncles, cousins, etc., all initialed."

"Strange, really strange." She shook her head.

"Well, that's what happened, but I'm not wedded to the tradition."

For some reason she pressed on. "What's behind the Codfish bit? I guess I'm taken by the absurdity...," she trailed off.

"Just keep talking," he told himself. "Codfish was a nickname given to me by my cousin, F.U. When I was a baby, F.U., a man taken to spirits, declared that it appeared that I had gills. Somebody ran with it, 'Yes, just like a codfish.' That was it. I couldn't fight my whole family. Everybody loved little Codfish."

She offered an insincere smile. "That's so incredibly stupid. I suppose you find it - I mean do you find it embarrassing being called Codfish or introducing yourself as Codfish?"

"No - I mean - yes. Hell, I don't think about it any more. I am who I am, right? Take all those people that get on television, you know, the ministers, the priests, the other liars, our so-called spiritual advisors. They say just be yourself, no matter what. Don't they say that? Or something like that? Anyway, I are me, Codfish Brac."

The girl chuckled. "Dear me, all this over your weird name. This is getting boring. You're on probation, Mr. Fish. Show me you're not a dullard."

Codfish could have jumped her on the spot but he clearly had work ahead to get to this doll. So he started. "Well, I guess we need the other side of the equation. Let's start with your name, rank and serial number."

"I'm Opal Vital," came the reply. She stuck her tongue out. "Yes, I hate my name, and yes, I have a nickname, 'Pooh.' However, I'll cut through the crap and questions and give you the Vital vitals. Understand I'm just being expedient. I just like to show my cards and see if it's worth continuing the game."

He shrugged, gave an encouraging nod, and turned up the corners of his mouth. "Great, let's play."

"I'm twenty-four years old, a graduate of Cal, smart, single, and unemployed." She rattled it off.

The word "pursued" should have been added to her short bio. She was chased, often shamelessly, and not just because she was a looker. Oh, there was that glory, but it was her fortune that was the magnet. What any number of men wanted to get their hands on was her money. And she had a lot of it.

Pooh's parents had gone missing on a Yukon back pack. No trace was found after extensive and expensive searches. The only child of bear food instantly was fabulously wealthy. As she grew up her fortune attracted good and bad people, but worst of all, money-hungry leaches of every stripe. Raised by a dingbat aunt, the girl turned out suspicious and fearful of men.

"Gotcha, any more vitals?" Codfish asked.

She gave him a self-satisfied smile. "I like to read and talk about things that people sometimes refer to as intellectual topics. I'm a patron of the arts. That sounds stuffy maybe, but it isn't. Anyway I am not bothered by a need to be involved with anything or anyone. I do as I wish. Like you say, I am what I am."

All this was said with kind of a steely sternness and Codfish felt he was tiptoeing over hot embers. "Well, we certainly agree on the involvement thing. I'm not and have no plans to be." He tried for a sincere, honest expression. "For the record here are my vitals. I, too, am a college graduate, San Francisco State. I like to think I'm pretty smart, but my guess is I'm not smart enough to compete with somebody like you, not that I would want to."

He chuckled and pushed on. "I'm in good to fair shape for a lounge lizard. So there, we have exchanged vitals. We're not quite a perfect fit, but then again we're sort of what you could call compatible, right?"

"You know show and tell?" she almost whispered.

He nodded.

"Well, buddy, I'm telling you I've shown enough."

Despite her twist to the negative she chose to play along for awhile. "The missing part of your vitals has to do with who you really are. Right?" She stared him down and continued, "But I'm not interested at the moment."

He nodded and wondered what to say. Pooh turned away and looked back down the aisle. A group of passengers had gathered at the rear of the cabin. Codfish rolled the dice. "Let's amuse our fellow fliers. It's something to do and doing is what I'm good at."

The girl nodded. "Okay, let's check out your social skills."

Codfish led the way as they walked to the back of the plane. He maneuvered with determined effort toward the small bar. The aisle was crowded and as traffic stopped Pooh she felt a hand on her arm.

"Hi there, missy, Happy New Year."

She turned her head and discovered two tiny, tiny people kneeling on their seats, facing backward. Not midgets, not dwarfs, these were scale model adults. The man wore a military uniform of some sort and his companion was wrapped in a fur coat. The ghastly thing looked like it was assembled from mole or possibly hamster skins. The little folk could have been fifty or seventy. Each had been victimized by a hairdresser.

"Missy, didn't scare ya, did I?" the little man asked.

Pooh was trapped - go back or deal with these two was the choice. Oh, well…she decided to turn on, "You startled me…the last stranger who touched me had serious finger problems thereafter."

The furry one piped up. "The Major is a hands-on guy. Just ignore him, honey. I do, have for years. What's yer name? I'm Twinkle and big boy here is the Major…his Christian name is Royd, but that's a secret." Twinkle had a super grin to go with her dancing eyes. Pooh was mildly fascinated by the tiny twosome but only to the point of wanting to stare.

Out of the corner of her eye she picked up Codfish heading back; he was struggling through the crowd balancing a small tray which held several full glasses.

"What's your name, dearie?" the Major asked. He licked his lips…constantly.

Pooh had gone this far, so what the hell. She leaned down and whispered in his face, "Sunfish."

The tiny couple exchanged one of those looks. The girl ignored it and went on, "This man with the drinks is my uncle, Codfish." Again the diminutive ones shared that look.

The booty was several plastic cups full of champagne. Pooh took two, asked, "Want some?" and then ignored the nods from the Major and Twinkle. She chugged one and started sipping on a second.

Codfish sent the tray toward the tiny couple and they each took a cup. Two were left. Pooh grabbed one and Codfish, left with the other, had a question for himself, "Does this girl have a drinking problem?" He soon found out.

"Uncle Codfish, tell these nice people how being so young and all, you're my uncle." She grinned and drained her glass.

"Why, yes, er, Codfish. Sunfish told us you're her uncle." The major seemed dubious.

A full bottle of champagne had been passed forward and pouring refills gave Codfish a moment of reflection or rather lie planning. "Yes, sir, I'm the last one of eleven. My oldest sister is my niece here's mom. See, sis is two score older than me." He downed his champagne and poured another.

Twinkle, with an insider's wink, nodded and declared, "Sunfish is pretty darn lucky to have an uncle that looks like you."

Pooh noticed that she was having preliminary control problems. She talked to herself as she bumped up against Codfish, "Jesus, this guy's pretty quick - and funny too. Of course, I'm half bombed." She eyed the major and asked, "Are you in the Army or Navy?"

The old soldier had a minor spasm, cleared his throat and gave her his official, stern look. "My dear, I'm U.S. Army retired. I'm presently the commandant of Custer Military Academy, Colma, California."

Codfish was immediately impressed because he'd been to a funeral in Colma - a town of few living residents and thousands of graves and crypts.

"You been in the service there, Codfish?" The major fixed him with a patriotic stare.

9

Codfish chugged, poured himself another, and then replied, "Seabees." Pooh smirked and offered a giggle. Her condition was either deteriorating or glorious depending on one's view of being loaded.

The major decided he did not approve of these people. He should not have talked to the girl; that was a mistake but, hell, a good looker always got to him. The civilian was probably a draft dodger. He made Twinkle turn down a refill as he went into a disengage mode. That was for the best as Codfish and Pooh had found each other. They bumped together, touched a few times and finished the champagne.

"See ya later," bellowed Codfish as he gently pushed the former Sunfish back up the aisle.

He turned her around when they reached their seats. The first, and several subsequent kisses were put into the category of momentary entertainment by the girl. Codfish, on the other hand, was in love, or so he told himself.

At this point in the tale Dad would usually loudly say, "Sonny, if it's not love at first sight, take a hike!"

The cross-country flight arrived in San Francisco at 5:30 a.m. Pooh and Codfish, who had dozed for a couple of hours, appeared somewhat dazed as they left the plane. They melded into the herd of hung-over passengers as it eased into the terminal. The young couple sort of walked together but Pooh was on a path of her own. He was caught short as to what to say. Finally he blurted out, "Could I have your phone number?"

Pooh kept walking, reached into her purse, pulled out her lipstick, stopped, grabbed his arm and wrote a number in vivid red on the back of his hand. She looked at him and said, "There, yes, in answer to your unasked question, I want you to call me sometime. And yes, I like you. I'm just exhausted so I don't want to talk, okay?"

The smitten Codfish looked at his hand and started to memorize the number. "Sure, okay."

As they walked up the concourse the girl decided to be nice. She turned to him and murmured, "Do you want a ride?"

"You car's here?" He was surprised.

"No, I'm being met…by a man."

He sighed, "I see…I'll pass on the ride."

She moaned, "Oh, God, another baby. Men are so insecure. Come with mama, I'll take care of you." She took his hand and led him toward a totally bald Chinese man who was dressed in dark purple, head to toe. Codfish locked on the purple sneakers.

This man was a presence. He was maybe five eight at the most, maybe two hundred pounds at the least. His neck was stacked layers of flesh. Codfish told himself, "This guy is scary, weird and probably not an act." He screwed on a weak smile.

The man gracefully walked toward them, reached for Pooh's bag and gave Codfish a once-over. "Welcome home, miss," he said softly. "Is everything all right?"

Pooh replied, "Yes, Noodles, I'm okay. This is Mr. Brac. We'll give him a ride into the city."

It was a huge Chrysler, not a limousine but big enough to hold a number of bodies. The girl was silent as they rolled up Highway 101 as dawn presented a foggy sky. The lame, undistinguished buildings of the Financial District and the handsome Bay Bridge were the ultimate clues that they were in San Francisco.

Noodles, in his quiet way, requested an address from his passenger. "Corner of Lombard and Van Ness is fine," came the reply.

A barely audible second question was whispered by the driver, "Don't you have an address?"

"Noodles, leave him alone, if he lives on a street corner that's his problem." Pooh knew her protector well as he had served her parents for years and had known her since she was born. She had learned some of her code of conduct from the imposing man. One of his little homilies went, "All men are suspect...your mind is your foil." That one took, it was her cornerstone.

Noodles whispered again but his voice carried to the back seat. "That corner has a couple of bars and a gas station. He probably lives over a bar." He was right as usual.

There was a bit of a production as the trusty man servant guided the huge car to a stop exactly in front of The Yellow Spittoon, a renowned dump of a bar. Noodles turned and said, "This must be it, right, Mr. Brac?"

Codfish grunted and looked at the girl who feigned sleep. "I'll call you."

No reply. He got out of the car, took his bag from the grinning Noodles and found himself speechless. Not so the other man, "Good luck, Mr. Brac, she really is impossible. One date if you're lucky." With that he turned, walked a few steps and climbed back into the car.

Codfish stood on the street for a moment collecting himself. He muttered, "Jesus fucking Christ." The door to his flat was next to the Spittoon and he let himself in, walked up a long flight of stairs and sought refuge in his undistinguished residence. He had a beer and thought about her, and tried unsuccessfully to sleep. The glorious Pooh haunted him.

Codfish spent that afternoon nursing a couple of bloody marys while he watched a stinker of a Rose Bowl on the tube. All the while he rehearsed lines and told himself he would nail her on the first call. Hell, why not now? Five rings, then a woman answered, "Vital residence, may I help you?"

"Ah, yes. This is Mr. Brac, I'd like to speak with Pooh please, Pooh Vital."

"Mr. Brac, please state your business. Miss Vital is indisposed."

"I see, I'm sorry. This is a personal matter. If you would tell her I called and will try again."

The woman replied, "Yes, do that." Then she hung up.

Codfish yelled at no one, "Bitch, goddamn bitch!"

It went on for three days. He carefully spaced his calls but made no connection with the girl. One call was answered by Noodles who sounded a bit sympathetic. "I told you she's impossible. But if you want to be driven crazy, keep it up, Mr. Brac, keep it up."

Noodles was right, he'd had it. Codfish went downstairs to the Spittoon where two hours of handling vodka on the rocks restored his self-image to the point that he staggered into the phone booth. He had a few false starts, especially getting the coins into the slot. "What asshole designed this piece of crap?" Finally he managed a connection, and there was a pick-up.

"Hello." Good golly, it was her.

"Hi, Pooh, this are Codfish, your former friend, wannabe lover, and public disgrace."

She laughed, "You sound like you're bombed. Are you?"

"Why not take a fucking call or one of several calls? I'm going mad, and I am mad, goddamnit. What's the deal?"

There was silence. He could hear her breathing. Finally she blurted, "Wealth is a painful blister."

"What's that mean?" he shouted, "I'm the one in pain." There was a catch in his voice.

Pooh said, "Look, it's about the guys I meet. I'm paranoid. I see somebody I like then fear starts. I'm scared as hell because I immediately think he likes me because of my circumstances or money - so I turn off."

Codfish felt himself sobering up - fast. He hoped, then guessed that he had her, "I'm coming over, where do I come?"

Another pause. She gave him the address.

So Codfish got started with Pooh. At least he thought that was the play. He had no allies, friends or other help. The target was always moving and not toward him. She lived in luxury, had tons of money and thought all men were after it, including him. She made that clear on too many occasions.

He chased Pooh; proposed all sorts of dates, adventures and whatever. She was interested...maybe. At least she went out with him. The girl withdrew when he tried to talk about the two of them, a relationship, something. His sympathy for her suspicious nature became tinged with a growing fear... was she wacked or maybe was he? Here was the orphaned beneficiary of trusts and the outright owner of a huge home in Pacific Heights; what's her problem? The girl's annual income was staggering or so he deduced. She had shared some details with him.

The money phobia had to be dealt with and Pooh was sort of on top of that issue. Codfish, whom she might like to be on top of, hadn't come the route of most of her tainted suitors. But so what? She still had to work through her paranoia. Did he have her scoped out? Was that flight just an accident or did he arrange the meeting?

Fortune hunting aside, there was the quality-of-life issue for the girl to deal with. Codfish was smart but not necessarily cultured. He had accumulated a store of general knowledge and a certain confidence in telling people about it. But he failed Pooh's assay and that was crucial. He had not been exposed to art, ballet, opera, or the symphony. Her message was delivered emphatically. These pursuits were her interests. He should learn to enjoy them. And he tried, but with the exception of the symphony this stuff hardly grabbed him. "This will not get in the way, I can take anything," he told himself as he sweated through the ballet season.

Codfish worked at an advertising agency and enjoyed a reputation as a young man who might really come on. The pay was low and he saw himself treading water in a way. Until now his avocation of sorts was fooling around with the stock market. His modest savings ended up there and over time grew a bit. The nascent capitalist couldn't help but learn something of the world of finance. It was the start of a lifelong intrigue. But now he played the comparison game; his bucks compared to hers was a dismaying contest.

Codfish and Pooh dated, made out with obvious pleasure and desire but he always stopped when directed. She told him, "No adventures below my navel, and that's that." The girl had a pleasure-giving attitude despite her declared and enforced no-play zone. She sent him away happy, at least for the moment, and that was her purpose. Set the hook and keep the shark at the end of the gaff. She had been taught to be nice as well as courteous, even to those less fortunate. And she was so nice.

More was on the table as it usually is when the chase is on. There was the terminal danger of boredom. You do fun things time and time again and sooner or later you question the fun. Codfish slid into self-doubt, "Am I wasting my time? Am I ever going to get her?"

He had been mesmerized for six months, but where was this going?

"Shit, nothing happens without hard work." He looked in the mirror while shaving. "Look, to get her, you'll have to kick some ass and that means her ass."

They sat in the paneled living room of her grotesquely unsuitable mansion. There was really no other description for it. Three ugly stories of stone concealed a magnificent space of interior. That is if you're into wood paneling, high ceilings, dramatic stairways, and marble. Marble was on the floor and completely dominant in the nine bathrooms. Codfish found the interior as warm as he imagined Lenin's tomb to be.

As a relatively honest fellow he told Pooh, "This is a place where you should live when you're ninety years old and somebody is wheeling you around. It has all the comforts of an old folks' home."

"What do you mean?"

"I mean this place is preposterous. Sorry, baby, it's too weird; it's a dump."

"Well, I like it, and this is where I'll always live," Pooh pouted.

"That's too bad. I mean living alone could be tough …if it's for the rest of your life." He glanced at her. She stuck her tongue out at him.

Codfish left after a shortened version of their usual lips and hands. Neither participant was into the flow. Pooh's last words were, "I like my house; it's not a dump."

He offered no further comment. "So much for ass-kicking tonight," he thought, "next time it'll be different." If he only knew.

She had grumpiness in her voice and a resident bad attitude which he easily read over the phone. What was it this time? Codfish was still catching hell about calling that dump a dump. This call started like so many other recent go-rounds. After his, "Hi there," came the deluge.

"I'm bad company, sorry to report." She sighed and went on. "I'm flat-out brain dead. I want to get out of here. I've been sitting around for months letting you take me on dumb dates while you bore me with vacant observations and half-truths."

"Jesus, Pooh, what is your fucking problem? If I bore you it's news to me. You just want to have a fight. I'm the dumpster because I'm here and you need somebody to dump on."

He paused and she came back. "Maybe you're right, dump, you say, maybe I should dump you."

Codfish felt fear in his gut and that was a new sensation as far as he and Pooh were concerned. "Hold on, Pooh, we need to talk…"

"What do you think we're doing?" she hissed.

"I mean in person, I'll take you to dinner."

He was surprised when she quickly answered, "Okay, but at a place with a tablecloth, not your usual coffee shop."

"Fine, I'll pick you up at seven." Codfish hung up.

"Fisherman's Wharf! How imaginative." Pooh was smiling at Codfish as he backed into a parking place.

She grabbed his hand as they crossed the street and held on until they went in the door of Crabs.

The greeting was a bit much. "Mr. Brac, we're honored once again. How are you, sir?"

Codfish managed a full-voiced, "Good evening."

"This way, madam, to Mr. Brac's favorite window table," gushed the host. This man was a walking definition of the word "unctuous." They were seated and Pooh asked, "How can you be such a fucking jerk?"

"See a tablecloth," Codfish replied lifting the edge and winking at her.

"So this is your favorite table; they love you here. Where have I been?" She was the sarcasm queen.

"It's all a joke. Cool it. We have the Crabs account, my boss did me a favor." Codfish laughed.

"Some favor, you looked like a kid on prom night. Do you have the crabs or what?"

He considered letting her have it but chickened out. "Come on, Pooh, climb down a bit. Let's have dinner without name calling. You can pick up again after desert."

They ordered and stared out the window. "A painful blister," she said slowly.

"Meaning what?" He grabbed his water glass.

"We're at that well-known dead end, that's what it means." She attacked a cup of glue-like clam chowder while keeping her eyes on the table.

He raised his voice. "Do I have to defend myself here? We're doing okay as far as I can see. Sure, we fight…everybody does. I see this as a great match, we

19

should end up together." He was trying to catch her eyes and finally succeeded.

Pooh put down her soup spoon and raised her head. She was not exactly burning him with her stare. "Look, I like you, Codfish, but I'm not in love with you. I'm sure of that and it won't change. There's no reason for us to continue on, that's my message."

He felt the sweat running down his torso. With all her shit, she'd never been close to this. "Let's take a break, think it over, not see each other for a couple of weeks." He pushed a bit of a grin.

"How about a couple of years?" Pooh, the bitch, had arrived. "Just take it like a man and take me home now."

The short ride was taken in silence. Codfish had to control his shaking hands by putting a death grip on the steering wheel. Pooh sat with her hands folded on her lap. She looked controlled and in a sense she was. The hardest part was over. When she dumped a guy there was always the question of the reaction. It could be anything, from tears to fears. Violence, suicide, anything was possible, at least she'd heard those threats. Her goal was to make sure the discard went away, away to stay. She had her plan for Codfish.

The course of that evening was hardly spontaneous. The girl felt the urge to free herself for a couple of weeks. That developed from the usual seed. The more Pooh thought about it the more obvious it became. Why would Codfish stick around for months without any real encouragement, any real sex, and any real chance? He enjoyed the good life that her money often paid for…he was really entranced with her money, if you thought about it.

"Servants park straight ahead." She wasn't smiling.

Codfish ignored her and drove into the circular drive. He parked right at the front steps. For whatever perverse reason he wanted her to get more pissed.

Well, that worked. She was out of the car and at the door yelling at him before he had taken a step. "Come on, Mr. Brac, you know where your car goes and you can stay there too."

He gave the biggest smile in his repertoire. "Oh, honey, I forgot."

"Don't call me honey. I'm not your honey, you're history." She went in and slammed the door.

Codfish went up the steps and lifted the knocker, a huge old thing that was probably stolen from some castle in Europe, and began a slow, steady knock. First the maid and then the rarely seen cook asked him to stop. He didn't. Finally from an upper window, a blond head came shooting out and Pooh let fly.

"Look, can't you get it? It doesn't work. We don't work. I'm not going to see you anymore. Don't keep knocking on the goddamn door. Grow up, go get drunk or do whatever you do when you've had a bucket of shit dumped on you. That's what this is. My bucket to you. It's brutal, but it's true." She pulled her head in and the window slammed down. Codfish almost felt like wiping himself off. He took her advice and headed to the Spittoon.

Pooh had a sleep problem. The reaction from her former boyfriend had been tame, and she sort of admired his scene at her front door. But the steel-willed young woman knew she'd read him right. It was not in her character to second-guess and those thoughts were walled off. She hadn't learned that the best built structures of the self-righteous have leaks. That night things kept jumping up at her, especially when her eyes were closed.

The conversation with herself wasn't exactly a chat, it was more a litany of declarative statements. Hours of turmoil led to several oft-recurring thoughts. "I'm right to protect myself and my fortune. I can't be too careful. Codfish Brac may or may not be after money, but I can't take the chance. I'm probably in love with him. I'll sleep on this. Shit, I can't sleep."

He sent her a contrite note and expensive cut flowers. The apology was sincere, loving and persuasive. The last lines said it all and he hoped she would read that far.

"I know that you don't want to throw shit on me; you want to throw yourself on me. Until you'll see me this note will have to do. I love you and I can take care of you as you'll see. Please marry me and make us both happy. We should be together forever."

Of course she read it. She memorized it. The first time around the note was crumpled and thrown in the general direction of a wastebasket. Pooh screamed, "You asshole, you'll never get it. What a loser." Then she picked it up, unfolded it and read the note again.

Initially smart people react the way dumb people do. If there is no time to think it's pure instinct. With a bit of time it may be different. Upon review, there is

often a different take. This was one of those deals that
changed with review.

The girl had a second night of toss, turn and
turmoil. She had no real confidant, there were friends,
some relatives, there were trust officers. Who could
she talk to? It took a couple of days for her to admit to
herself that, yes, Codfish was the one to turn to. The
grandest sense of relief overwhelmed her. She took a
long nap.

She called him at work. His agency, Luger-Booger
Cosmoswide, had just landed a line of canned foods as
a client. Codfish was put on beans, a speak-ad
campaign. His creative juices were not flowing. Oh,
you know what immediately comes to mind, flatulence,
"Beans, beans, a work of art, the more you eat the more
you fart." He said aloud, "Please God, one inspiration,
I'll be a better person for you."

His phone rang. "Brac."

"Sweetheart, you've got to help."

"What's wrong, Pooh? This is Pooh, right?"

Silence. He tried again. "Pooh, are you okay?"

"Not exactly."

"Well, can you tell me?"

Another long silence. She spoke softly, "Codfish,
you're the one. I think I knew it on the plane, I just
didn't…"

He interrupted, "I'm coming right over."

She said, in what appeared to be her normal voice,
"Don't forget to quit first, if you want to. You'll never
have to work on anything but me…ever again."

He took her advice.

Pooh's attorneys constructed a prenuptial agreement which Codfish signed after running it by a lawyer friend. His pal warned, "Did you see this paragraph eight? You have to have your balls cut off and handed over to her lawyers one day before the wedding ceremony."

Codfish didn't care what he signed. He did try to read the thing to see if his balls were on the line or whether there was any other significant commitment of his body.

Pooh wanted and got a huge wedding. A planner was engaged, leaving only the all-important invitation list to the young couple. Codfish only needed some fifty slots leaving two hundred for the girl. She gave the nod to her many friends, her parents' friends and all degrees of family relations, liked or not.

Codfish stayed away from the endless arranging and caught up with Pooh's war stories at the end of the day. As he told her, whenever he got a word in, "All this is fascinating, babe, but my mind is on your melons."

Why six attendants each? He never got a satisfactory answer. The planner, Michelle Groth, could nod with the best of them. Talking was another matter. Pooh claimed that six was a magic number to the Romas. He asked, "Who's a gypsy for God's sake?" The groom-to-be came up with a best man and four ushers, including Bracs P.U., A.A. and Z.P. Now what to do? He didn't ask her, Codfish just asked him.

"How are we today?" was said with a big smile from the young man.

"Superb as always, Mr. Brac, is there something?"

"Uh, Noodles, I hope you'll be in our wedding."

The large man peered at Codfish. "You mean at your wedding."

"No, both Pooh and I hope you'll be an usher." Here was his first lie using her name, many more would come.

Noodles rubbed his forehead, paused, and then whispered, "I see that I must accept. Please tell Miss Opal."

Codfish thanked him and scurried to get to the girl first. "I love the idea, sweetie. Sure you were right to make it a request from both of us." Codfish had the first of many soft landings.

Guests and the wedding party were assembled easily. And so was Grace Cathedral, a bastion of WASP liberal thinking. The Vital family stood firmly on God's side and made sure all bets were covered by very generously endowing the Anglican Church and its programs. After the untimely deaths of Pooh's parents her trustees followed the trust's commands and gave on an annual basis.

They got the bishop, the boy's choir and the date requested. Michelle Groth was not as fortunate at the venerable Fairmont Hotel. This undistinguished pile was only two blocks from the cathedral and was the obvious choice for the lavish wedding dinner. The problem was the date as the grand ballroom had been previously booked. A gourmet sausage dinner was to be served to four hundred junketing proctologists. Michelle, upon learning of the conflict, put on her sexiest dress and went to see Luther Ludwig, the hotel's catering manager.

These two had been fencing for years. Luther, while a smooth operator in many ways, stumbled and often fell in his pursuit of women. Michelle thought him cute in an odd way but decidedly pathetic.

"So why can't you move those plumbers into two or three other rooms? That will work." She knew she looked like a hooker and guessed that's exactly what the creep went for.

He crudely inspected her and gave a little snort of pleasure. "Tell me, lovely Michelle, why don't we ever get anywhere?"

"What are you talking about? I bring you lots of business." She uncrossed her legs slowly.

"Heh, heh, maybe so. There's other kinds of business."

"You cooperate, give me the ballroom, and I'll cooperate."

"When?" He was almost panting.

"Is it a deal?" She stared him down.

"Okay, but when?"

"When this wedding dinner is over, when the last dance goes bye, bye."

He started erasing in his huge engagement book. Smiling like he was brain damaged, Luther got out, "This is superb, you won't regret it, Michelle."

The wedding planner took her leave with a confirmation letter in hand and a promise to herself to leave the wedding dinner midway through the proceedings. And she did.

That dinner, the wedding and indeed the whole day became a fond touchstone for the bride and groom. With memories galore it was difficult to single out a favorite, but Codfish did. He had sort of kept his eye on his seventy-two year old uncle, F.U. The drunk mink farmer damn near killed himself dancing every dance. He threw down straight shots of Fernet Branca as he sort of steered his partner of the moment by his table so he could grab another. To the groom this was Brac outrage at his best.

Pooh loved her wedding in that society met her husband's advertising colleagues, assorted friends and strange relatives. New allegiances were born which she guessed would last at least a week or two. More than a few of her friends mentioned the number of people who went by initials rather than names. Pooh had the same answer to all such inquiries, "Codfish's family is name deprived."

Two years later Pooh and Codfish were playing with a baby boy who is me. I'm blessed by my parents with the name of "W.T. Brac, Jr." I was and am called "Sonny." I never really cared for my name but what do you do?

Mom and Dad spent an unusual amount of time together. In fact, a day worked best when they spent hours talking, reading, and spoiling me. Still Mom had her charities, the Junior League, and many friends. Dad was now officially an investor, which gave him license for long lunches with new and old frauds.

"I was goddamned near ruined by money," Pooh mused.

"Until I came along." Codfish tried to grab her but she giggled and slid away on the long leather couch.

They were in the billiard room, one of Codfish's few hangouts in the huge house. I was on my way toward the glory of being totally spoiled. At the moment I was playing on the parquet floor.

"I don't want Sonny involved with money, mine or what will be his, until he's grown up. Then he can deal with it and sink or swim." Mom fixed her husband with an intense look.

Codfish thought a moment before he spoke. "You can't avoid who you are. You're rich, for Christ's sake. We will raise our boy as well as we can, but he's going to be bathed in dough no matter what. Hell, what can he think being raised in this dump? Unless we're careful he'll have more servants than friends. What we do is try to raise a nice and responsible rich kid."

"You show me how, big boy." Pooh got up, turned, took a step and then jumped on him. Codfish yelped and put his hands in play. They shared a long kiss and then an electric look. Pooh mused, "I'll call Nanny if you like."

They were naked, on their backs, holding hands and talking. She was again harping on the curse of wealth. The recurring message was tempered with her rejoinder that her husband had rescued her from her plight. She meant it, loved him so and would have been at peace, more or less, except for worrying about me.

Her child couldn't go through what she had…she had to make sure. Pooh turned on her side resulting in an unintentional erotic pose. Codfish tried to grab a feel and got his hand slapped. She spoke with a serious tone, "Honey, I want your promise, your oath…if anything happens to me, you won't let money ruin Sonny." She stared at him.

"Come on, sweetheart, don't be morbid. Nothing's going to happen to you. You'll always be able to whack Sonny when he needs it."

"Promise?"

"I promise. Come here."

I was a mischievous ten-year old when I had to help Dad cope with the unexpected. Mom went down to stay, the victim of a rapidly working cancer. The graceful and beautiful woman left a grieving son and husband and a fortune.

The late Mrs. Brac had an estate plan which paid Uncle Sam his due, more or less, and left almost ten million dollars in trust for me. Dad got the dump and two million. Several charities and the University of California, split a few million more.

Dad saw to it that I was spared detailed knowledge of my wealth…I would live as I had - which was extremely well. Codfish, a seriously depressed widower, took to drink and unfettered swearing. The man perfected the use of countless funny, disgusting and raunchy terms. This manner of speaking, he pretended, was a living tribute to Pooh. And lotsa fun.

CHAPTER 2

The gorgeous brunette had to be six feet tall. If there was a visible flaw, and many would call it a compliment, it was right between her shoulder blades. Tonight's dress hinted at reverse cleavage as the back panels got together just outside her kidneys. The front was high and tight. This costume, an electric blue sheath, was calculated, with her very deep tan, to package a real big deal which is how she privately referred to herself.

Partway down her lightly muscled back was a black mole which was oblong, hairless and the size of a giant jujube. She had no problem with the congenital spot, and save a select few with whom she had decided to share it all, the mole was not seen unless she was in a bathing suit or dressed to show. Tonight she showed.

She was part of a group of four men, all in various states of open admiration, and another woman who was the caboose and not enjoying it judged by her surly, turned-down mouth. Each had a drink, a napkin and varying degrees of anticipation. They had adopted the usual cocktail party stance. One of the men had deviled egg stuck in his moustache. Nobody had bothered to tell him.

The party celebrated the launch of the latest ego massage for a recognition seeking rich man. This time money was thrown at the peculiar world of magazine publishing.

As the rich man's lawyer, friend, and son, I'm rather involved with the always unpredictable W.T. "Codfish" Brac, Sr. Dad is the rich guy, so they say. I'm so much richer there's no comparison, but that's my business. Codfish spends and Sonny doesn't.

I was sitting on a rock-hard wing-tip chair not ten feet away from the gorgeous young woman and her male harem. I moved into that position to get a better view and enjoy a clandestine stare at the exceedingly well-built, tall lovely in blue. I shifted my body arrangement as the chair began to eat my posterior and my shorts attacked my privates. Detraction helped my discomfort so I concentrated on musing what could be done with and to the brunette. I interrupted myself and turned my head, almost by instinct, as Wally Moundminer crept into the suite.

Wally was a decided jolt to the eye, but those self-anointed experts who later said that they immediately marked him as an outrage were guilty of misdemeanor I-told-you-so. At that time I didn't know his name or who or what he was. That would change.

The man was unconventional appearing; his scabrous but well-tailored suit was a shiny lavender. He wore greenish suede shoes and carried a white cane. The fraud was not sight impaired as it turned out. Wally was reed thin, quite tall and not that bad looking if you caught him from the right angle.

When I spotted him, the oddball did not at all appear self-confident. He had eased into the room with darting eyes down and a grimace on his chiseled face. Wally took a moment to find his target and then headed, on a direct path, to the bar. His movements were anything but cautious as he waved his cane and charged ahead. He jostled several arms and deliberately shoved one tiny, older woman aside. It was a rough passage indeed. This rudeness was picked up on by most in the vicinity but nobody that I saw spoke up. The suite was jammed by this time, so while Wally made a decided ripple, his presence did not appear to be a big deal beyond the small circle of new enemies he had quickly made.

My position in the punishment chair gave me a fine panorama. I was against the wall, between two windows and able to see most of the room, quite a few faces and lots of female asses. On the right stood the graceful package in blue and on my left the bartender. I was set until she moved or I was.

Wally's mumblings became clear speech as he plowed up to the bar. "Excuse, sorry. May I please have a double gin lolly, hold the lolly."

"What?" The bartender looked up at the tall man.

"Look, my dear man, pour gin in a glass, large glass, if you please, some ice also, if you can."

There was a sneer and scowl from the barman as he looked for his smallest glass. No more than an ounce of liquid hit the ice. Wally smiled at the glass and drained it.

"One more, if you can." Momentarily, he looked pleasant enough. But then the bounder handed the glass to the barman, wiped his mouth with the back of his hand and burped with great vigor and resonance.

That stopped things in that corner of the room. Wally, by a clever rolling of his eyes and a nod of his head, convinced some observers that the barman was the culprit. He quickly got his second drink; the barman privately prayed for salvation and asked his divine to "Strike this shithead dead here and now."

The prayer went unanswered and the lavender-clad man moved in front of me toward the beautiful girl. This was done by putting his greenish suedes on both of my Italian glove-leather loafers. He noticed the unevenness of the footing apparently because I received a look, a smile and what might have been the start of an apology. His words were cut short by another loud belch.

I mouthed, "Pecker-neck."

Wally, now a bit glazed in appearance, drained his drink, smiled and replied, "I'm really downtown… forgive if you can. Here's my card, call me and I'll make it up to you."

I then received what appeared to be a claim check from a shoe repair shop. This came out of a jacket pocket of the lavender suit along with some crumpled money and two rubbers. All of that hit the floor; he ignored it.

Wally ended our brief encounter and locked a stare onto the tan back which was a few feet away. Because I was trampled by and involved with the flake, and because of my lust for the owner of the back I was looking at her when it happened.

Wally suddenly switched demeanor. He squared off and looked in physical control. A serious, professional mask took over his almost good looking face. He looked like a gentleman, a man of substance and grace who was about to undertake a mission.

He smacked her with his open hand. The mole was the target. Whack! The beauty fell forward and her forehead struck the open mouth of one of the gawkers. She bounced back a bit and I saw that the splendid face had decided toothmarks along with some blood and deviled egg scraps. The man she struck slid to the floor yelping.

Wally shouted, "Sorry, I was just trying to get that horsefly on your back."

I was frozen for a moment as Wally took off shoving his way through the crowd. There was a hush in the room but it was soon broken by a long, loud belch. He shook up and down his entire body. The bastard was laughing. Wally left the party without looking back.

I stepped into the mix and was introduced by somebody as the publisher's lawyer. My interests were decidedly non-professional and I hoped to somehow make that clear without leering.

"This is Bergen Bode...Sonny Brac."

I mumbled, "Can I do something for you?"

"Just a minute, I'm a mess." She had grand brown eyes which were filled with tears. The previously ignored and petulant other woman had found a role as nurse. She dabbed away at the bruised and littered forehead while assuring, "It will be okay, Bergen. That man is a beast."

"A son of a bitch."

"A real shit."

"Goddamn fairy."

The whole corps joined in.

I stared while my mind sought clever words - a string of them. Nothing came. The cries of the outraged softened a bit and Bergen wiped her eyes with an admirer's silk pocket hankie.

"Now talk, jerk," I said to myself. Too late.

He came through the crowd trailed by the magazine's editor who was engaged in what was likely a losing battle to stay on under Dad's new ownership. Dad was a polite man to most and tonight he had arranged with himself to put up with any and all bullshit. He worked the crowd, paused to acknowledge greetings, shook a hand, patted arms and shoulders and stole an occasional peak down any dress that looked promising.

Codfish at fifty-four was at the top of his game. Starting at his top there was a balding pate home to substantial patches of greying, fine hair worn combed straight back and into a modest ducktail. The hair was the crown on a large head which wore a round, pleasant face. All this was mounted on a short, thick neck which was attached to a rounded but solid two-hundred pound body. While there was a certain crudeness about his size and shape, the package broadcast a sense of physical and financial power. He dressed as well as money would allow. And that was damn well.

Dad, not unlike most of us, had a few character traits that made him somewhat distinctive. Take Codfish, the nickname he relished and always used.

The absurdity was hardly lost on the man, but that made it so useful. He had a way of rubbing his forehead when events called for a bit of a retreat. "Why, shit, old Codfish isn't going to screw you or anybody else," he would ooze as he slipped around trying to acquire some business, thing or body on unfair terms.

Dad's behavior was greatly influenced by his belief in the power of direct communication. He'd spout, "No crap, that's good enough for me." No rules counted except his. English grammar was given ambivalent treatment. His forte was swearing, with an emphasis on the vulgar. This was part of the act, but it was constant so perhaps not all that contrived.

Here's Dad on vulgar language, "Christ, I just kept going and the more people noticed and commented, the more I fucking cut loose. Your dear mother, bless her, had her way with this lingo. I learned at her knee or was it the other way around." He chuckled.

Dad reached Bergen's group and before saying a word, aimed his large hand toward her upper arm. It looked to me as if she turned toward the gesture. He patted away and smiled up at her. "Howdy, Codfish Brac is my name. I admire your work."

The heavily perspiring editor, Fenton Hadley, jumped in. He sported a tweed jacket with leather elbow patches, black corduroy pants, pipe smoking regalia, and saddle shoes. The voice was cultured and soft. The magazine under his reign was awful. But, looks counted to Codfish, and if Fenton looked like Dad thought an editor should look like, he might stick.

Fenton, murmured, "W.T."

"Call me Codfish, damn it."

"Yes, err, Codfish, please meet Bergen Bode. She is one of San Francisco's most admirable and recognized models. Her specialty," he became instantly sly, "is lingerie."

Bergen gave Fenton a dazzling up your's smile and turned toward Dad. I rapidly became a mere spectator and could only blame my frozen state of a few minutes ago.

Dad grabbed her offered hand with both of his. It was an interesting troika as Bergen had finger length to rival most men's aroused members and Dad had the width and size of hands uncommon except among certain primates. A delicate pattern of fingers tipped by claw length nails stuck out from the oversized sandwich made by Dad's hands. He held his grip for a long moment. "What the hell happened, my dear? I heard the commotion."

Bergen looked at him with some intensity as I saw it. Then she sort of whispered, "Not much until now." Oh, boy.

Dad's mind functions quickly. His eyes swept the onlookers, returned to our little group and settled on me. "Sonny, find out what this was all about."

I sort of nodded. He looked again at Bergen. "Nobody here is man enough for you, let's go."

She grabbed his hand and they went across the suite together. They brushed through the gawking crowd, looked directly at each other. Dad looked angelic as he peered up at the beautiful face. He was in for a crick in his neck.

* * * * *

The note was on the center of my desk. I was in my law office on Sansome Street having just arrived at the usual 10:00 a.m. Not bad for a guy who's been practicing for all of four years. Because I am rich, notoriously so, and know most of the right people, I have and get clients. I can call the shots most of the time and get to the office when I want to.

This law firm, of which I am a principal, consists of a small group of malcontents who fled large, established firms. Most of my colleagues live off of referrals and individual clients. There is a passive recognition that barring the unforeseen, nobody here will make big bucks the way we practice law. The upside is if you marry you stay married to your spouse, not the law. We work civilized hours and try not to represent shits.

In a way, I am the future of our firm. I bring in business and more is bound to come. This is a very nice way for me to establish myself as I send most of the work to my colleagues and still get a piece of the fee. For myself, I take only those clients and matters which I care to with one exception. And in that case I'm on call, always on call.

My practice involves representing Dad. Not that he wants much help or lawyering. But he can use me so he does. He's had and has a series of "investments" and getting in and out of these adventures sometimes calls for labor by my fine hand. When he bought LIVE magazine a couple of months ago, I was his buffer. The seller was a wealthy woman from a formidable, old San Francisco family. Her incredible cheapness and stupidity finally ran the rag into the ground a few years after her publisher husband killed himself rather than come out of the closet.

That was a scandalous happening as Sedgwick R.V. Drainwasser was a "man's man" who spent many of his drunken evenings denouncing, "The fucking faggots who've taken down this great city."

But Mr. Upstanding was really just one of the boys. Finally disgusted and beaten down by hypocrisy and gallons of scotch, he ended his long liaison with the doorman of his club. Sadly that was not all that he ended. The publisher kept going when others prudently turned back during the annual ocean swim by members of the Fogg Club. He left a note dumping on Mrs. Drainwasser.

> "Had you seen your way clear to cleanse your face of those weird oils and salves, we would have spent our nights in the same bed. I would have had you and not been forced out into the harsh, animal world of men only. I am ashamed and so should you be. Rastus."

The ghastly widow was not the least bit shamed although she faked it for awhile. She wanted, and got, lots of condolences, invitations, and attention. Everyone tolerates a rich widow and some even favor the species. Hortense Drainwasser took over her husband's holdings and pretended to listen while lawyers, accountants, investment advisors, and relatives, massaged her. She ignored the lot and dumped her fortune into Mexican highway improvement bonds. That is, everything except LIVE Magazine.

The magazine was her toy for a few years until she sold it to Dad. I handled the sale negotiations with her lawyer, Philip P. Phillip, known as "Three P." A decent enough guy, he happily gave me the word according to Three P. "When this is over, I'm rid of her, save the annual total rewrite of her will. You can guess why that happens. Some relative hits the skids so he's out. Somebody else doesn't return a call that costs, etc. etc. My client is very difficult. Mrs. Drainwasser does, however, mean a great deal to me. Assuming I get the probate of her estate, she will mean a great deal indeed."

"Practicing law can be damn tough," I said.

He gave a solemn nod of agreement. His eyes did the smiling.

The note on my desk was on Dad's stationery, light blue with a black band around the edges. A small logo of a smiling cod was embossed and centered at the top. The message was typed by Barbara Boring, who was anything but. She was Dad's weird secretary. Dad operated out of our home, a remodeled ferry boat which was moored at Pier Three on the Embarcadero. He sold our family home, make that Mom's mansion in Pacific Heights, three weeks after she died. "I can't stand this fucking place," he announced to me, his ten-year old grieving son. He emphasized that this had been his sentiment from the day he first set foot in "the dump."

On our way out Dad gave each member of the household staff a generous severance payment. He could be the salt of the earth. Old Noodles, still going, got Mom's Chrysler and twenty-five thou.

The Aardvark had earned her living hauling people and cars on San Francisco Bay. Put into history by the bridges, the ferry fleet disappeared. A few boats survived and Dad scored one. Renamed, restored and elegantly redesigned inside, it became our new home and a part remained as Dad's office. The new living arrangement soon worked for me although my kid's ego was degraded since we moved from a mansion to a ferry boat.

Barbara's typing was flawless, I scanned the note.

"Sonny: A reminder from last night. You do remember last night? Find out about that fuck who hit Bergen. I am meeting with staff at 2:00 at mag office. Be there - sober. Dad."

This gives one an idea of the kind of crap visited on me, a highly respected member of the bar. However it takes me only seconds to restabilize after a tiny ego wound. Without Dad's business, I might be defending indigents, working for some government, or living off my inherited wealth. All of these options are unacceptable. So, whatever the Codfish wants or needs, I'm his man. And, despite the antics, he is a solid guy with a thoroughly entertaining grossness.

My call to LIVE's offices wound its way through three female voices, the last one purred, "Annette Andersohn, may I be of assistance?"

"This is Sonny Brac calling for Mr. Hadley."

"Thank you, I'm Mr. Hadley's assistant, what can I help you with, Mr. Sack?"

"Could you please get Mr. Hadley on the line?"

"I am very sorry, he's indisposed. Perhaps I could help."

"Miss, uh, Andrews—"

"Andersohn, that's s-o-h-n."

"Sorry. Look Miss, uh, Miss, I need to speak directly with Hadley."

"Mr. Hadley will be returning calls at 4:00 p.m. May I put you on the list, Mr. Sack?"

Me, of the long-burning fuse, reached the end. "Madam, that will not be satisfactory. I am due in surgery at 2:00 p.m. for a penile implant. Have the dear chap give me a ring. It's Sonny Brac, same last name as the new owner." I heard a bit of a gasp before I slammed the receiver down.

Except for the purchase negotiations and attendant due diligence, my contacts with LIVE had been limited. Hadley was my best and only source for a possible ID of Bergen's horsefly killer. Having wished that rationalization through my brain I abandoned the project for the time being and concentrated on lunch.

My health needs require a measured amount of drink per day. It's a given that self-diagnosis will save mankind. My treatment is refined as it has gone on for several years. I drift on sort of plateau of sauce. I usually drink with lunch, often during the afternoon and definitely before and during dinner. After that I'm set up to pass out in or on the bed. Life on the plateau has numerous shortcomings, not the least of which is that women usually grow tired of me fast. That keeps me single and unhappy and it seriously threatens the legitimate succession of my branch of the Brac family. So, I'm going to have to put myself under review. The question is when?

Most of my lunches start with a bloody mary. Then wine or a beer helps with the usual sandwich and fries. Evening cocktails are booze of any stripe. When dinner is on some table or another I'm ready for wine. After that I'm more than ready to fold. This pattern varies with circumstance and the severity of my ongoing hangover. When I fall from the plateau into the depths I cut back or even abstain for a while, but these are temporary measures. My system, I've lyingly convinced myself, functions best when I am controlling myself by drinking.

Dad, who has paid more than his share of alcohol taxes, has given me regular warnings about booze abuse. These started when, at sixteen, I was deposited at the pier front after a nasty vodka bout with two twenty-year old touring hookers from Latvia. Superb young ladies as I recall. Home in the arms of our faithful watchman I puked on the Codfish just as he opened his cabin door to see what the noise was all about. He recoiled, called me a "miserable donkey's putz," and told the man to tie me up on the Aardvark's deck. The guy knew who paid his salary. The next day was my first temperance lecture. Even with rope burns it did not take.

Now it was lunch time once again. Our law offices were in a tired building on the corner of Bush and Sansome Streets. Half a block away was the joint I loved, needed and spent dearly in. I hurried across the street against the light, grabbed a paper, and made my entrance into the Iron Duke. Onto a bar stool, I ordered a bloody and a french dip. This got me started...I followed habit and scanned the early edition of the afternoon paper. I moved to a glass of vino, ate a bit and settled into my cruising configuration.

From the Iron Duke it was a five or six block walk to LIVE's offices on Mission Street. This was a pleasant way to try to settle the mess in my stomach. Downtown San Francisco, the Financial District that is, as it spills over to south of Market Street, is fairly well policed. A few winos and homeless types are around; then again, how many are a few? In this mix are the bottom feeders who are subject to an old-fashioned roust if the cops are feeling pushy. There are plenty of men in blue available to take on these defenseless bums. The Chamber of Commerce has point men all over city government, and it dictates who gets the services. Downtown comes first.

I walked on relatively clean sidewalks and looked at the girls. The warm, sunny October weather had brought out superb female costumes. Christ, does anybody but me consider how many great tits there are? Delights, one and all. A horn blasted in my head, "Life isn't all boobs, Sonny, you're going to work."

CHAPTER 3

LIVE was on the second floor of an unfortunate office building in the middle of an unfortunate block on unfortunate Mission Street. The erection could have been fairly new but it looked tired and decrepit. The faux brick facade was painted urine yellow. That alone was enough to discourage a second look. The tenants who cared to be found were listed in the small lobby. I read the directory:

Blackberry Patch - An Experiment in Massage - 3
Budd, Elmo, Ginger, Oski & Teegrr, Attorneys at Law - 4
Pen-A-Trate - Motion Consultants - 3
LIVE Magazine - 2
Thomas, Nader and Ashcroft - Refuse Analysis - 5.

I knew the lawyers, or rather of one of them. Angora Ginger had one of the loudest mouths in San Francisco. Need a useless opinion about anything? Just ask her or don't bother, she'll spout no matter what. This legal strumpet was a publicity hog of startling poundage. Lawyers are generally despised by the public, wonder why?

I walked upstairs past chipped grayish walls while carefully avoiding the badly tarnished bannister. The LIVE office entrance was as plain and uninspiring as the halls which it faced.

Inside the door the atmosphere and look were a refreshing change from what I'd just walked through.

Ex-owner Hortense Drainwasser had an interest in decorating so it seemed and she was not too reluctant to pay the prices charged by those darlings who do interiors. So she wasn't necessarily the cheap old mess that many called her. However she was a troublesome mark because decorating money flowed, if, and only if, she made the selections...of everything. A smart decorator learned to "preview" a Hortense expedition to the wholesalers and dealers. The client was firmly pointed to where the conspirators wanted her to spend. She unfailingly took the bait.

Hortense's taste ran to modern modern, at least when she decorated the offices of LIVE. The result looked like something out of a furniture showroom in Finland. Wood and glass dominated the space. The walls were covered with expensive Belgian linen which added much-needed understatement. Lighting was track with large Scandinavian-style fixtures hanging low over desks and work areas. Colors, as might be expected, were bright splashy yellows, reds and blues. To my eye, this was a good effort. After my first inspection, I was pleased to the point of telling Dad that, "This space is great, we can forget spending any money on the offices."

He rejoined, "This place sucks."

The office took half of the building's second floor. There was an austere reception area, large conference room, several individual offices, an all-purpose room/kitchen and a library. I scored big by suggesting that the library be converted into a bar. Dad's response was a resounding "Fuckin a." I found the furnishings utilitarian, but Dad's problem was with the big picture, "I want this crap sent back to the Baltic on the first available steamer." He appeared serious. "Hire a contractor...we need a bare knuckles newsroom look around here. The only export from Scandinavia that matters has two legs, walks around and looks like she just stepped out of a toothpaste ad." The subject of office decor was closed.

I stood inside the door and eyed the receptionist, a very attractive recent graduate of Stanford whom I was to learn was named Dede Figueroa. The doll gave me a friendly look and pointed to the conference room. "They're in there," she said, somehow speaking through what must have been a permanent smile. Great teeth, and the rest was sensational based on my quick inspection.

Dede was either too eager to please or suffering from a muscle disorder around her mouth. I filed her under "future investigation I should, but probably won't make." I crossed in front of her desk while giving her a complete up and down accompanied by my studied half-leer. I was so pathetic but her large unblinking, brown eyes played at innocence. I swear she sucked in her stomach to accent her very adequate chest. The smile never changed.

A bit disarmed, I tripped slightly on the thick, hooked Icelandic wool rug and started to fall. This was one of those stumbles where you propel forward, slightly off balance, but there is little danger of going down. A reflex grab at Dede's desk gave me a tentative handle on a plaster sculpture which was the head of a woman. I swept it onto the carpet where it shattered.

"Oh dear, Mr. Brac, you've broken our Neri," Dede looked a shade whiter than the plaster components lying on the rug. She murmured, "It cost a great deal, I know, are you okay?"

"Sure...fine...thanks. What do you mean, 'our Neri'?"

"Well, Mr. Brac, your father bought this sculpture, other art, furnishings and everything. I mean, when he bought LIVE he bought it all. So it's ours, er, yours, you know? Didn't you do the deal?"

I skipped an answer to that, collected myself a bit and then took another good look at my latest sex object. Dede was not a large person except as noted earlier. She glowed in that California blond, tan sense, the exploitation of which sells lots of lousy movies, horrible TV shows, and questionable consumer products. The previously ever-present smile was on vacation - she looked serious, concerned, and in need of my comfort and attention.

"Would you like to join me for a cocktail once the meeting is over?" Did I noticeably drool? "We can conspire on how to hide the fact that I broke this formerly magnificent piece of sculpture."

She offered a questioning look, then a smile, "Sorry, but my husband is picking me up right at 5:00."

She didn't hide it. She enjoyed that line. Where the hell was her wedding ring? Her hands were naked except for a large gold ring with a dandy piece of jade inset. I leaned over and helped her pick up the pieces and fragments of the sculpture. As I headed toward the conference room I tried a clever rejoinder. "You're lucky to be married. In this town, men are either married or gay. There are very few eligible guys. A single girl has a tough time."

She looked right though me. "Which are you?"

"Eligible."

"Well, you might try to get in touch with yourself. You may be lots more than that."

Whoops, what to say? I grinned, and went into the meeting.

Dad sat in the position of power, even though the table was round. He accomplished this by shooing away anyone who tried to sit next to or even close to him. This meeting was what Codfish called, "The Big Flush."

Dad bought LIVE effective October 1 so the October issue was on the newsstands and November's was almost ready to go. It was the usual drivel. There was no way to help. December, the Christmas issue, would be fat with ads and holiday hoopla. That, too, would be left alone. Dad made January the target for his regime to take editorial control and put out a product which was a screeching change of course for the magazine.

The conference room was an impressive space, with windows facing out to Mission Street and a glass wall facing the working part of the office. Hortense Drainwasser had let the round laminated birch table and purple stained wooden chairs make her statement. The walls held some reproductions of lame billboards promoting the magazine along with a collage of various covers of LIVE. One, "Finding Normal Sex in San Francisco." caught my attention. I didn't remember reading that issue and made a mental note to do so.

The staff was sitting in various nervous postures. This was, as Dad had told me earlier, "Pants shitting time for these jack-offs. Most fear for their jobs...and that's highly reasonable considering..." He had trailed off.

Fenton Hadley was in his editor's costume. The smoke from his pipe had seriously fouled the room even though somebody had opened every window. I heard later that when Dad had entered the room the first thing he said, albeit with a grin, was, "Fenton, put that fucking thing out and never show it in my presence again!"

Fenton had coughed, mumbled, fought the crimson creeping over his ears, and left the room taking his pipe and accompanying equipment. He returned shortly empty mouthed and handed.

Next to Fenton sat Worthy Feckheimer, the art director. Worthy was hard to figure. He could have been thirty-five or fifty-five. He had a classic look starting with his crown of short, combed-forward hair which was worn in the popular greek style. The clothes were update, update. Everything for appearance was the man's credo and while one might question black sheen as an everyday basic color, you would not argue that this skinny, little fellow did not spend big boutique bucks.

The business manager occupied a chair and plenty of table space. Directly in front of him were stacks of bound somethings. These were government green binders which looked as important as the federal budget or some other tome of great significance.

These were probably financials and related documents. Those are things that many look at, few understand and none master…including the authors.

The formidable pile was guarded by a guy who looked the role. Gary Paul Freier was an "accountant's accountant" as he would brag whenever possible. When pressed the man's little trick was to use German phrases to put off potential troublemakers.

Codfish was busy giving Gary Paul's massive pile of bound paper the fish eye as everyone settled in.

"Who's missing? Anybody?" Dad smiled around the table.

"Just Annette and Wally," said Fenton.

"Say what? Find the miscreants," Dad loudly ordered.

Everyone avoided looking at the publisher. Dad was making sounds; he was growling as a matter of fact. There was undisguised apprehension in our little group.

"Uh…Annette Andersohn is my executive assistant. I'll get her." Fenton grabbed a phone and pushed the intercom button. No answer. Again his ears started to color. Everyone was looking at him, watching him, and he felt the heat. The editor started to twist in his chair giving unintended body motion to his dilemma. He launched an angry assault on the phone buttons. Still

he fired blanks. In an act of grace in roared Annette.
This lady had no problem asserting power. Large
people usually don't. She was big, not really fat, just
big. "A sumo wrestler without the gut," I thought.
"Stay far away from this one; she breaks limbs."

"Please sit down." A nice Codfish smile
accompanied his greeting as he pointed to the chair next
to him.

"Where's Food and Beverage?" asked Annette.
She'd noted the absence and decided to try and suck up
to the jerk publisher.

Dad, oh so softly asked, "Why was my invitation
ignored?"

Fenton collected his thoughts and lied, "Wally
Moundminer, Codfish, is quite ill."

Dad nodded and muttered, "The poor lad."

The meeting was on and the great man held forth.
"As you may know, I have no particular background in
publishing. I have not been associated with magazines,
slick or sick."

Nobody smiled so Dad did. "But my late wife often
said, 'Codfish, if you get a chance to invest in
something like Mechanics Illustrated or Boy's Life do,
that would be a meaningful use of our money. We can
help spread culture to the masses.' She said some other
things too, which I can't remember. So in her blessed
memory I purchased LIVE. Now, my question is how
can we use this stunted organ for the enlightenment of
our fellow man? What say you, Ms. Andersohn?"

Annette expected this about as much as she
expected a proposal from Jane Fonda. Taken aback,

she cocked her head a bit and started opening and closing her large mouth. Small flecks of spit came out, no sound; she cracked her knuckles. Finally, a basso, "I am not qualified, please. Mr. Hadley is our editor."

She gave a quick glance at the Buddha grace of Codfish and then shot an imploring stare at Fenton. He coughed his way to a rigid, upright position and launched a rehearsed speech. "Mr. Brac, ah, Codfish, on behalf of the editorial staff and, of course, the business side, I am delighted to welcome you as LIVE's new owner. A short, but important historical review is in order in that our roots are basic - they are this magazine. We who are blessed with the opportunity to serve her always remember her heritage, the trials of our predecessors, the…"

"Tra-la-la, Fenton, you can put that trash right in the dumpster with most of the past editions. They are synonymous, the same, equal - garbage." Dad smiled happily. Fenton reeled and colored badly again.

Dad pressed a bit. "I simply asked what we can do for the enlightenment of mankind. Anybody?"

No takers. Fear had dropped in. This bastard was crazy and mean. The pregnant question was, "How do I get out of here?"

My head was starting to ache and I pictured a long, unfair but entertaining "Big Flush." The plan for the meeting was Codfish's alone. He had only mentioned that he wanted to "talk turkey to the insipid leaders of the staff." However, I got the hint.

"Here's the vagina for the meeting." He smiled again at the cowering audience.

One rarely experiences dead silence in a room containing that many people. It existed for a moment or two, then Dad's secretary, Barbara Boring, crawled out from under the table. I had not noticed her. Had anyone else? Perhaps not, there were gasps and frightened looks. It's safe to say that legs crossed and sphincters tightened.

Dad handed some papers to Barbara and she distributed one to each of us. Passing by me, she whispered, "You'd better wake up." I was the last recipient and as I got the paper I saw that it was entitled "Agenda or Vagina, Take Your Pick."

1. Pledge of Allegiance:
   W.T. "Codfish" Brac, Sgt., U.S. Army (Ret.)

2. Invocation:
   Rev. Annette Andersohn, Dyke-o-Rama.

3. Financial Report:
   Gary Paul Freier, CPA, Business Manager, Fraud and Embezzler.

4. Editorial Report:
   Fenton Hadley, linguistic pervert and pipe-sucking wimp.

5. Art, Style, Make-Up & Make-Out Report:
   Worthy Fuckheimer still has a job. Please appear in black-face from now on, we're weak on minorities and you'll match your clothes.

6. <u>Food & Beverage</u>:
   Launch death star for Wally Moundminer,
   Food & Beverage Editor.

7. Resignations accepted.

8. Remaining bums fired.

9. <u>New business</u>: This magazine is now named
   LIVE/DIE.

10. <u>Benediction</u>: Sonny Brac, Esq., Chief
    Counsel, Owner's son and heir.

Bedlam. Tears, especially from Annette as she struggled to her feet. The chipmunk cheeks were wet but the jaw was set. She threw the agenda, now a handball sized missile, at Dad. He ducked and it harmlessly hit Barbara in the chest. She reflexively brushed off her boobs. Annette swung toward the door, stopped short and shouted: "You bald shit, you're cruel and petty. Fun at everyone's expense. Christ, I'll get you...get you good." She started sobbing.

Dad smiled and looked my way, "Give her the hook. Does everyone know that Reverend Andersohn has routinely given this magazine's story ideas to our competitor? She passed any intelligence her fat ass picked up, to our beloved rival GOLDEN SHOWERS. No comments? This sausage has a big interest in a certain broad at GOLDEN SHOWERS and that's why that crowd scoops you jerks on the few good ideas you have."

Annette whirled toward the glass door, missed by a panel, and walked straight into safety glass of the finest grade. She may have broken her nose, we never found out, as she groped her way out and into history.

I tried to catch Barbara's reaction to this - were they soul sisters? Would Dad pay for his crude carrying on? He didn't give a flying fornication, so why should I? Barbara was mute, her head down.

Paul Freier screamed, "I've been libeled. I'll sue the socks off you! I demand my severance pay now. I demand my salary...I demand...you *tittenfick*."

Dad was standing and uncharacteristically yelling, "If this company that you fundamentally controlled had the right insurance, among other things, the fidelity bond carrier would be here with handcuffs. We have to rely on other ways to recoup since you've never bonded yourself. So, we've kidnapped your wife and sold her to some Iranians, friends of the late, great Shah."

"What? For Christ's sake, you are sick...rotten. I *moechte einen Anwalt anrufen.*"

"They said she was damaged goods, and she's been returned. So our only recourse now is to take it out of you. You say you want to call a lawyer? Go ahead, Adolf. Our bill is sixty grand, as you well know. That's the amount you've stolen in the last eighteen months. That being the total time of your tenure at LIVE. What do you suggest?"

Gary Paul moved toward the door. He looked as if a very important part of him had left his body. The color, such as it was, had drained from all his flesh that showed. He was starting to sweat in great quantity… the guy was barely hanging on.

Codfish helped him out with, "We'll take cash, no credit cards though. This enterprise is learning from the biggies. You buy gas with cash and what's good for Richfield is good for us. Or something." Codfish sort of bounced. A happy man. He did a short shadow-boxing number. Paul was gone.

The conference room was an emotional refuse dump. I rested my head in my hands and wondered what was next. The "Big Flush" was akin to a high school theatrical. Each character had his or her turn on stage but continuity was meager as it was supplied only by the lead thespian, the one who could act. The cast members came on, did their bit and then left. There was limited interchange. The extras stared, mouths in various corpse like poses. It was heady but decidedly not enjoyable. But one continues to learn. I was amazed that our leader understood German. Dad told me later that the first word crudely thrown at him meant tit fuck.

Worthy was crying without a sound that I could hear. I was just across the table. He wiped his face on the sleeve of his shiny black turtleneck and stared at the floor. My guess was he fought to stop his modest display from becoming an all-out blubber.

"Worthy Talent" was his nickname when he was a student at the San Francisco Art Institute. He was facile and that was it. He sort of absorbed the basic techniques of the various artistic disciplines. The problem, which he knew seemingly from the very beginning of his pursuit of art, was a dearth of talent. Originality missed his sailing. He had tried it all. Even the great crutch of a camera didn't work. Worthy Talent was a cruel nickname but what did one expect from a bunch of art students?

Worthy watched and copied the styles of dress affected by successful artists and film types. After trial and error he settled on glistening basic black - "No, I don't wear pearls," he steadfastly would reply to barbed questions.

Worthy's potential for success was further crippled by his lack of confidence. Self-criticism and doubt had made him honest, but in a world of phonies it was suicide. With his quickness he might have been a successful untalented artist, or perhaps a critic. But neither scam was his because he couldn't pull it off. At thirty-eight, he barely made a living trying to stylize a small, regional magazine with limited financial and talent resources.

Worthy wiped his eyes and cheeks with his black, silk handkerchief. His mind wailed, "This brute is so awful. What has he got on me? I suppose he'll start on homos. Jesus, Mrs. Drainwasser hated me - I was the kind that supposedly ruined her husband. She said that to Fenton. Wanted me fired. I need this job. I need the money. Goddamn it, it's not fair."

Dad was back in his chair. "Is there anything to drink around here?" he asked of no one in particular.

Barbara, saying she would look, left the room.

Dad again, "Just us boys."

Worthy looked scared. He was thinking, "Here it comes."

"I'm inclined to keep you two if you care to stay. There is going to be a new alignment, of sorts. This soon to be great organ is about to change its format to compliment my brilliant name change. I'll give you a preview and then you can decide if you're sticking or parting.

First, as our president often says, 'You get what you pay for.' That's why our beloved leaders' salaries are so low and why so many jokers go into politics. Anyway, all salaries of LIVE/DIE staffers will be increased by fifteen percent on November 1."

Worthy thought, "That's it, I can take this puke, no matter what."

Dad leaned back, put his shoes on the table (he was wearing fawn-colored penny loafers) and checked out his small feet. "My people have analyzed this operation from a business and editorial standpoint."

"What people?" I asked myself. Then Codfish floated yet another surprise.

"The business side is simple. We lose money, lots of it. But the one recoverable charge is the dipping of that Fascist Freier. I have instructed our general counsel - wake up, Sonny - to avoid the embarrassment of having the slimy shit prosecuted. Right, Sonny?"

I nodded and gave Dad a solemn look. This was all news to me.

"As a gesture of my contempt, I've arranged for the publication of the following in tomorrow's paper." He handed out some proofs:

LIVE/DIE MAGAZINE
will be closed on
Columbus Day
in memorium
<u>Gary Paul Freier</u>

"Jesus, Dad, he's not dead. This is libelous. It has all kinds of ramifications. You mean they'll print it?" I was horrified.

"First, they think our boy is as dead as Chiang Kai Sheck. Second, let the little motherfucker sue; he is too scared to go pee pee. Third, I can't be a publisher unless I libel people, even if it's in some other publication."

Fenton was blinking rapidly. Would he speak? No, a little raspy throat squeak was audible, but he was not about to deal with the maddened Codfish.

"Thank you for your unanimous approval. Here's another tidbit, in more ways than one." He winked at me. "The business side of our enterprise is now in the capable hands of our only Stanford graduate, Ms. Dede Figueroa. Now, I know you may think this appointment odd, or rash or whatever but Dede is a smart little trick."

I flashed to myself, "Say it isn't so, you horny father."

"My people learned that she was a business theory major at Stanford with a minor in corporate revolution. She's well-suited for her new assignment. Dede has accepted the position as business manager and assistant to the publisher."

I was now slipping toward the posture of Fenton and Worthy. Blown out. Often people do not hear all that someone says. Were we hearing all of the Codfish message? This was a three-cornered presentation in a four-cornered world. He was roaring away. I was confused. Too fast. Too much. Who were "his people?" How did this happen? Was it happening? I slapped my face. Too hard, damn it.

"Need a belt, Sonny? Ring for Barbara." He pointed to the phone.

Nobody moved decisively. I sort of tried. Fenton lifted a hand and turned to reach for the phone. He fell short. We were not functioning well. Barbara appeared at the door and Dad gracefully went over to slide it open. She carried a tray with two champagne bottles and plastic cups. Dede was behind her.

They sat down and Dad continued. "Pour that stuff, please; welcome Dede." She smiled at everyone.

"Congratulations," I managed. Was she doing Dad? "Quite a surprise."

"Indeed," said Fenton, trying still to figure out the circus.

"I am so happy to be joining you in a different capacity." This was a very self-possessed and luscious young woman. Dede gave me grace, "Sonny, all that was a joke." There was that smile.

What was a joke? Was the sculpture a fake? Was she married? Was she smiling at my puzzled

61

expression or just at me? Do you get a complete body charge once in a great while? I did right then.

The Codfish was prowling around, sipping champagne. Wound up again, off he went. "Now editorial. Fenton, it would help so much if you'd change your name to Fenwick." He manufactured a dramatic pause while he stared out the window. "Just kidding," he chuckled. "No, I'm not going to kick your arse anymore; you've done a fairly good job with what you have to work with. One question?"

"Yes, Codfish."

"Do you ever shit in your hat?"

Fenton boiled; he struggled out of his chair. "You're crazy. One at a time you take good people on for the fun of destroying them. I do not and will not play your preposterous games. Keep your magazine, your raise, your in-house whores."

Dede threw her champagne - it mostly missed Fenton but caught Worthy in the face. Out came the black silk hankie;, if this kept up it would be soaked.

Fenton and Dad met at the door. The fist went deep into his stomach. It was a low blow; the editor went to his knees and collapsed on his side. A classic embryo. Dad had to drag Barbara away. She had jumped up and was kicking the moaning editor. I think she caught him in the thigh. Well, how to get this straightened out.

Dad's love of combat did not equal his love of women but it had a certain priority in his scheme of life. He fought rarely, as far as I knew, but there was a real vengeance when it occurred. I had witnessed a few nasty episodes over the years and rarely did things go beyond Dad's first punch. He was very careful not to tangle with anyone close to his size or the least bit dangerous in appearance.

I pulled the still moaning Fenton to his feet. He was gasping and heaving. "No, no, not here," I prayed. I helped him out into the reception area. There we stood together like exhausted marathon dancers. After a minute or two the editor seemed to breath almost normally.

Dede came out of the conference room, sliding the door closed behind her. She had a serious look and held a check in her hand. She gave it to me. "It's for him," she also said more with her eyes than I had time for. It was hard to do anything with her around. "Mr. Brac says it's his severance pay and blood money. Get him to sign a release of all claims before you give it to him."

She looked at me continuously. This was five star eye contact…and I vowed I would get on with the rest of it.

I forced a glance at what she gave me. I held the magazine's check made out to Fenton in the amount of seventy-five hundred bucks. On the explanation stub, there were various entries but "purpose" caught my eye. "Services rendered - fun and games."

Fenton was sitting on the reception room couch looking none too spiffy. He copied our conversation and asked the question, "How much?"

"Seventy-five hundred."

"Write out the release, I'll take it."

I smiled down at him. "Okay, but first…this may seem somewhat irrelevant…but in a way I'm just as disturbed as my father. I need an answer."

He nodded vigorously.

"Who was that guy who pounded Bergen Bode on the back at the cocktail party?"

Without a pause he said, "Oh, Christ, that's Wally Moundminer. Read the masthead. The wine and cheese editor."

I sat down at Dede's desk. There was a small silver-framed picture of a man sitting on one corner. The subject looked like a young Marlon Brando. I was jealous! This began to hurt so good. I drafted the release in a few minutes and asked Fenton to read it and sign his claims away. It was a fast read, even for an editor. His hand quivered as he picked up a pen and signed. I handed him the check and he headed back to his office to collect his things.

Dede caught me looking at the picture. She purred, "My little brother," while she laid on an innocent look. Whatever the play I was not in a position to do a lot. This kind of female collision had occurred to me on occasion and I usually drank myself out of it. That is to say, and it bears repeating, my drinking ruined my relationships with women sooner or later. Sooner happened when some lovely scared me. Sooner was rapidly approaching.

"I'll see to it that Fenton leaves without setting the place on fire," Dede said.

I sighed, "Okay, what about the meeting?"

"Nobody's left for Mr. Brac to play with," she smiled again.

I went back into the conference room. Barbara and Dad were finishing off the champagne. Worthy was a shrunken black lump in his chair. He looked like a bird cage with the night shade lowered. Codfish and his secretary appeared to have been chatting; they looked quite calm.

"Did he take the check?" Dad asked.

"Automatic."

"Well, I'm truly sorry that things didn't work out. Fenton has an opportunity to earn a living as a pugilist. Right, Worthy?"

"Er, may I leave, please?"

"Certainly, see ya later alligator." A big crock smile came from the publisher.

Dad's feet came up on the table. He'd taken his shoes off. His hands folded together on his round stomach. Here was a man content; his digestive juices had worked hard as he ate up all those poor people.

I told him, "The guy you want is Wally Moundminer, he's your wine and cheese editor."

Dad's plastic cup hit the table with a hard click, "What guy?"

"The guy who hit Bergen."

"I want to talk to him, asap. What, pray tell, does the wine and cheese editor do? This magazine is a fool's delight."

"We'll find him, that is, your people will find him."

Dad grunted.

CHAPTER 4

Roy Inciser had values, even a personal philosophy if you want to call it that. None of this was very complicated but the man was reluctant to discuss or disclose what he really thought or believed. Since it was all in his head and he spoke guardedly one had to guess where Roy came from. Take his analysis of the interminable political meetings he attended. He would disappoint almost everyone who participated as they thought this part of the process meant so much. People who considered themselves informed or current as well as those who pretended insight into the game usually believed that a political campaign was much more complicated than it was. This considerable cadre of self-appointed experts would spend hours around dinner tables, over lunch or just about anywhere discussing their suspicions about a given candidate and why so much emphasis on such-and-such issues was right or wrong or whatever.

The "science" of the opinion poll was their leading crutch. But how easy it is to say that polls show people are in favor of clean government for example. And so what? It's crazy not to start with the candidate, rather than the issues. That was Roy's belief, philosophy and credo. He lived by the old saw, "It's the spokesman not the message."

And when it was done right, it was image of the candidate that would win the race. And with limited exception, only a modest amount of substance was ever flashed. Roy held most candidates in contempt. These person versus person beauty contests just didn't do it for him.

Now campaigns that really tested skill, he might tell you, were those that hit voters in the pocket or pocketbook. Even more challenging were the measures that wrote a special interest program into law. Initiatives, referendums and the like were the lifeblood of political consultants and their lamprey. All too often the electorate was persuaded to vote for an outlandish proposition because of clever, deceitful campaigns which tugged on the sleeve of alleged community need or a sympathetic cause.

The San Francisco Endorsement League did its part to further electoral decay. Roy Incisor was the League's press man, executive director and general staff know it all. Among other things, the unimposing man was an undisguised cynic, a trait necessary to keep him afloat in the turbulent political seas.

The walkup had one flight of straight and rather steep stairs. On this block of Second Street was a row of dumpy buildings which dated from the Twenties. Progress in this part of downtown San Francisco meant remodeled space going at modest rent. Storefronts in buildings of two or three stories housed non-descript lunch joints, cheap jewelers, clothing discounters and the like.

Above Milldue Brothers Jewelers were the offices of the San Francisco Endorsement League. The League space was for rent, or parts of it were, to campaigns and candidates which the organization liked and endorsed.

These arrangements turned on the dollar. The League voted to endorse based on how much it was offered for the favor. That was not a policy meant for public consumption or even known by most League members. League membership came from representatives of a cross-section of the City's establishment. Business, labor, educators, churchophiles...some forty odd in total. It was a decided honor to hold a seat on the League even if it meant, and it always did, being a rubber stamp. A thoroughly awful candidate could become the League's champion if the rotter agreed to rent space and pay a fee toward defraying League advertising. And the same went for ballot measures.

The League endorsed, bragged with newspaper ads, and most important, mailed a slate card to every registered voter in the City. Expensive? Yes, but the candidates and advocates paid for it. There was a carefully prepared budget, although it never had a line item for surplus. That was not a subject for open discussion as the League banked a handsome secret profit which went to its dynamic co-chairmen. Roy Incisor was in the middle of this scheme, and he got his bonus accordingly.

Second Street had joined the rest of the City in basking in an early October Indian summer. Leaving the bright sidewalk and starting up the musty, poorly lit stairway was not a happy transition. Monte Footbound grabbed the outside door handle and got ready to leave the sunshine. He rubbed his beard, ran his hand through his thick, tightly curled hair, sighed, did it again, and started up the stairs two at a time. Not bad for forty-one. He made the top without much heavy breathing.

He took a sharp left, smiled at the secretary, and stepped into the only enclosed space in the loft. Wood partitions came up a few feet, then glass extended to the high ceiling. The room was narrow and long and it comfortably held the ample furnishings. Campaign posters covered the walls and a large photo of the League membership hung on the wall. Monte closed the door.

League meetings were brutal, especially listening to all the red-vein marked veterans tell it like it was in their day. But today was an executive session. To any inquiry the response was "personnel matters." For once that wouldn't be a lie, not today.

Monte was late as usual, and the looks he got suggested disapproval. His silent rejoinder was, "Fuck 'em." He had spent his lunch hour at a porno flick palace on Market Street. Today's show was titillating even for a regular and one thing led to another so he was late. With a weak smile he slipped into a chair.

The room was furnished with a large desk and a long worktable fitted to it forming the letter J. A random collection of chairs were scattered around the table. Seated at the desk was the undistinguished and disarmingly young-appearing Roy Inciser. He had been laughing and was still smiling at the two men seated at the table when Monte plopped down. B. Overland Nicely was dressed, head to toe, in the conservative blue theme he felt fit his position as City and County Republican chairman. B.O. sat across from a short, stooped little man who had a shiny bald head which totally dominated his small body.

The notable head belonged to "Topper" Bello, Chairman of the Democratic Party in San Francisco. At seventy-two he was not in good physical health, but his famed mental process was intact. Topper lived for politics, his private fixation was to see his personal wealth substantially increase at each election. He was rarely disappointed.

Topper owned the Topper Club, a successful bar and race book in North Beach. The club made some money but that was gross. After expenses, make that pay-offs, profits were good but not great. Topper's big bucks came from his interest in two massage parlors. The old gent was a silent partner, so to speak, in these whorehouses. Silence did not preclude auditioning a new masseuse before she got a job. He was partial to oral massage as a job candidate was carefully reminded before an audition.

Topper was looking at B.O. Nicely with his lizard look. With eyes half-hooded and his tongue circling around his lips the little man made studied, quick nods of his bald head. B.O. had just remarked that he suspected a modest amount of money was en route—that brought Roy's laugh just as Monte slid in.

"Hello, gentlemen, sorry I'm late."

"No problem, Monte." Roy's smoothness was in need of a sincerity dose. "Drink or something?"

"No, thanks." Monte gave Roy an insincere smile.

B.O. was the agreed-to spokesman. "Yes, um, Monte, the entire board of the League met last night as you know."

There was a nod from Monte and an obsequious look. He hoped that was the read he gave. Monte just despised these assholes.

B.O. strove to be Churchillian. "This is a sticky one, Monte. Topper and I got into it—not with each other, mind you—but there's an element in the League, which I'm afraid is growing, that opposes progress. These pansy pluckers would see our beloved City of St. Francis stop in its tracks, stop right now. No more growth, no more progress, no more new good for the general populace…"

"You're right as always, B.O., but hurry it up, I've got to go." Topper had to audition a new Vietnamese sister act and that was causing him no small amount of anticipatory palpitations.

"Yes, yes, hold your water. So, Topper and I spent over one hour in debate. I'll make it short, we triumphed. We got the sixty percent needed to endorse —barely. So it's "Yes on Q," thanks in no small measure to the two of us. It was, if I do say so, damned difficult and I know you'll take this message back to your people. Nicely and Bello take full credit for this."

Monte put on a serious face. He spoke softly, "Gentlemen, I know everyone will appreciate your efforts. Now I have a cashier's check here for $100,000 which is to pay for advertising and support from the League for 'Yes on Q.' As usual, the co-chairmen are the payees."

Monte gave the check to B.O. who caressed it before carefully handing it across the table to Topper. After the co-chairman's blessing it was passed to Roy Incisor. The press man tried to look nonchalant. He failed. Roy looked like an eighteen-year old in possession of serious contraband.

Monte got up, shook hands and backed out the door. B.O. clapped his hands and chanted, "Yes on Q...Yes on Q."

Monte, bag man for business, the establishment, what have you, had made the delivery. The final good-bye was unexpected, "Right on," yelped Topper.

Monte's exit called for a drink which the remaining trio lapped up. "No chit chat about our friend," B.O. calmly said, "He knows too much...he goes." He nodded at Topper. What Roy didn't get, and how could he, was that B.O. was talking about him.

"Uh, Roy, we're in perilous times here. Right, Topper?"

His co-conspirator nodded and poured more for himself. B.O. had his usual quart bottle of ginger ale which he had attacked without pouring into a glass.

B.O. belched and continued, "It's cash flow really ...we're cutting back and your position has been eliminated. We just don't need a press man."

Roy managed, "What the fuck are you talking about?" He was whiter than usual.

"You're gone, dear friend...here's a thou separation pay. You'll have the finest recommendation." B.O. pushed a stack of money toward the flabbergasted Roy.

Roy took a few seconds and then stood up. "I see it as a matter of trust - you don't trust me. I've got loyalty up the ass for the League and you two know it. What's the real reason I've been canned?"

Topper oozed, "Roy, I'm personally going to match that grand. So there. Now, I've gotta tell ya. Some of our best friends are afraid of you, or really your integrity. Things are going to be rough this time, you're too good a person to be involved."

Roy yelped, "It's that pervert Monte, isn't it? I told him early on that Prop. Q would steal mother's milk from babies and I meant it. So the cocksucker bought my job. Right?"

Nobody spoke.

"I'll take your blood money because my family has to eat. This stinks, you both stink. Lucky for you I'm not the type to hold grudges," Roy smiled. He was an accomplished liar.

* * * * *

Their trip across the hotel lobby was theater of some kind. It was a little after seven and the LIVE/DIE crowd was well-oiled. The lobby bar was full as the invitees had spilled out of the party suites and into the public rooms.

Harlet House was one of the City's top hotels. It was chic, small, and planted firmly on top of Nob Hill. An occasional conventioneer with knowledge would book, but the Harlet was not a convention hotel and it did not solicit or accept group business. This was a place for the rich, pretenders, and the highest class of hookers. Codfish Brac used the Harlet for small entertainments and occasional trysts.

Tonight's party had way too many invitees, free loaders and working girls. They should have been in several suites instead of the two which the publisher had insisted on. Codfish was pissed off and looking for someone to yell at when he met Bergen. In a flash he was no longer upset or even thinking about the launch party for his magazine. The girl had a way of taking over. Consider him taken.

The new twosome turned heads and drew comments both snide and supportive. The young woman in blue was "so hot, I could cry."

"She's so much taller than the big guy, he must be her body guard."

"It's her father, they're holding hands."

"The horny old devil."

Codfish and Bergen sustained their vision duel. They had not said anything except an occasional "whoops" or "sorry" since they left the LIVE/DIE party. By mutual consent, good sense and luck they traveled close together, held hands, got to the elevator and blazed across the lobby. Primitive attraction was at work, and that made it all the more exciting.

They were finally separated by the necessity of fitting into the small revolving door. Codfish was more than ample for the space allowed in one of the door's cubicles so it was separation time. She went first, turned around, walked backwards and smiled at him.

Codfish pushed slowly forward, grinned and felt better than he could remember.

On the sidewalk, blasted by the wind, he swung her to him. The first kiss was a natural. She crouched, he went up on his toes but not for long. Bergen had her "man to woman" technique. "When a man goes to kiss me, I will almost always be taller. I've learned to start out at about equal height, I then stand up gradually - he tilts up. He then assumes the traditional woman's position. He's kissing up just like most girls do. It takes no time for most guys to adjust. Hell, I'm worth it."

Her tongue was busy inside Codfish's mouth proving just that. He backed away; his neck felt strained. Laughing he went back for more. Bergen gave it and started to bite. By now they had attracted a bit of an audience and the doorman was grinning broadly as he held the door to the black Buick. He sent them off with a "Woo-eee."

Codfish pushed her into the car and said, "You're a carnivore." He was turned on.

"I'm not anything of the kind. I'm just trying to make sure you get my message."

"Which is?"

"Herpes."

He snorted and roared, "The boat, Willie." The silent driver swung smoothly onto California Street and headed down the hill toward the Embarcadero.

The couple in the back seat could not leave each other alone. Codfish, while an active lover, was not what is sometimes labeled adventuresome. He was a self-described "straight shooter." Not much went into technique. Over the years his interest had evolved into being serviced. Yet, he claimed to be sensitive toward a woman's needs, and felt he had not performed his role unless the lady "got hers" as he put it.

Well, Bergen was just not satisfied with old school sex, or any school sex. Her body was self-explored and adored starting when she was in grammar school. She had an interesting and orderly progression toward getting it all down. By the time she arrived in San Francisco from her childhood home in Vancouver, she was a fairly good model with marvelous natural looks. Before the girl reached the City she had had sex experiences with eight people, separate affairs or incidents involved her minister, one member of the British Columbian parliament, five school boys with high school or college pedigrees, and one sorority sister.

Bergen might say—and did—that she "honestly liked sex." Now at age twenty-six, she was careful not to let need take control. The object was career management—through sex if necessary.

San Francisco was an odd choice for an aspiring high fashion model. Advice from all the sources she could find in Vancouver was unanimous. New York. Go to New York. She got the message. But her plan, carefully thought through, called for something a bit beyond modeling. She wanted money. More than that she wanted wealth. She was raised in a family which lived on a very limited budget founded on a civil servant's salary. The Bode family was okay but that meant only that bills were paid and there was an annual camping vacation. The house was rented, the car always old - the clothes, the food, all was on the cheap.

The beauty's plan for wealth led to San Francisco because she wanted an open field, little competition. "Gosh, modeling will start me. There have to be a few available rich old farts in San Francisco."

She put her head on Codfish's shoulder as the driver smoothly maneuvered into the pier front.

The girl told herself, "This is too much. He's something; maybe even in bed. And he's got to have big bucks." She bit his ear lobe. He yelped.

"I've never done it on a ferry boat," Bergen laughed.

Codfish had struggled out of bed. He stood naked in the salon working on drinks. "In the history of the Aardvark, you're the first woman who never said no to anything."

"You mean since you've owned it."

"Owned her."

"Okay, her. Anyway, this her still wants more."

CHAPTER 5

Anita Lundberg, formerly by marriage Anita Farley, and in another long past marriage Astrid Kialt, was born Astrid Keller in Stockholm in 1921. Her path to San Francisco was intricate and full of intrigue - a story told elsewhere in its entirety. Life almost accidentally brought her wealth, and that status explained her lifestyle as she started on her sixth decade.

The woman lived exactly as she chose in a large, two-storied flat with high ceilings, plenty of light and understated decor. The magnet was a view of San Francisco Bay which stretched from Alcatraz on one end to Treasure Island on the other. From her roof deck a vista of Telegraph Hill and North Beach unfolded.

The handsome woman had lived on Russian Hill for decades. When her last husband left "for our mutual good," she stayed where she was with the singular goal of raising her daughter, Astrid. Anita had long ago decided they would not move from the flat until something or somebody came along which would make it worthwhile.

Anita had a cool look to her, some would say cold. She couldn't and didn't hide the fact that she still was a drop dead beauty. The woman was remarkable physically as she had the figure of someone much younger. Sure it was her genes, but little was left to chance. Aging was fought viciously. Her glory started with eye-catching red hair. It was natural, a gift from her mother and grandmother. Now, a few grey invaders showed up but they were quickly dispatched. A modest fortune was spent on beauty treatments, hair, nails, massage and dietary additives. She loved mirrors, that is when the reflection was hers. The woman constantly studied her face and body searching for a flaw or suspicious place. Her self took so much of her time. So what, what else did she have to do?

Of course, there were other matters which caught her attention. Anita followed her investments with a sharp eye. It wasn't that she could not tolerate reverses of fortune, it was that she had to blame someone if there were losses. Quite a bit of her money was in Switzerland and blaming those bankers was next to impossible. But in San Francisco brokers and bankers came and went. As did lawyers, apothecaries, suitors, and the like.

Dismissals were pleasant but firm. "Sorry, but I've changed my direction, I'm moving my business."

"We're not going anywhere, are we, so let's stop seeing each other."

The lovely-appearing woman did not get serious with men or care to. She had female friends or rather acquaintances, but none were considered close. The focus was on her daughter. Astrid got a full ration of her mother's attention - it was not exactly smothering, just careful, loving and watchful. This made it easy for the girl, who through college and medical school at UCSF lived at home and did so now.

Astrid talked to her father, saw him, and had an easy relationship with his second wife, whom her mother labeled "the yellow horde." Anita never adjusted the score after she was abandoned and she only had caustic words for her ex-husband and his replacement wife.

Anita found Sonny Brac through her bank, which was also his. It was an opportunity for recognition from both customers. So V.P. Horatio Fang made calls, set it up, kissed some ass and felt just fine, thank you. He purred to Anita, "We highly recommend Attorney Sonny Brac. While young, he is well-regarded and a prominent figure in the community."

"That's nice, is he a good lawyer?" she said with polished snideness.

"I can assure you that we at First American Reserve Trust think most highly of Mr. Brac as an attorney and, of course, a gentleman."

"Thank you, Mr. Fang, did you say he is expecting my call?"

"Yes, I was informed that his secretary will arrange an appointment for you."

"Thanks again."

She dialed immediately after disconnecting the insipid banker.

An appointment was scheduled and two days later Anita found herself in my law office, checking me out.

"Please sit down, Mrs. Lundberg." She was striking to say the least.

"Thank you."

I was rocked on my heels. The woman was pretty spectacular but her companion, left in the waiting area with a magazine, was a knockout. "A redhead who glows," I mused, although I didn't get that full of a view as I ushered the older edition into my office.

"Mr. Brac, I need your services, or at least a lawyer's services. I am impatient always so you'll have to bear with me." She had a smile which was meant to melt hearts.

"Yes, ma'am. I can adapt most likely. So it would seem we're at the purpose of your appointment. How can I help you?"

"Are you, Mr. Brac, familiar with or I should say I'm told you have experience in matters of money, of finance."

I suspected I could handle this. "Yes, as a lawyer and personally. Obviously I'm young, perhaps not seasoned you think, but the subject of finance goes way beyond practicing law. I take care of millions of dollars, by that, I mean I hold and manage millions. I take it you're in need of some sort of financial counseling?"

She crossed and recrossed her legs - a natural act but watching from the other side of my antique partner's desk, I found it damn provocative.

"I am going to consolidate my assets. I have accounts in Switzerland which must be dealt with. I have a portfolio there of stocks, bonds, and cash. I want to move all of it here. It's just too far away. I will not go to Switzerland myself. I need an agent, an attorney, I think, to handle this little move."

"I see. Is there a reason for the third party? Are you trying to remain anonymous or something?"

"No, nor will I be avoiding taxes or doing anything illegal. My accounts in Basel are old…they've existed for many years, decades. Everything about them is stale. Maybe I could go myself; the past may be irrelevant. Still, some people know I bank there. They, those people, may want to talk with me. This is remote but in any case, I do not want to talk to them. I want you to get my money out without creating a stir. Bring the proceeds to San Francisco. I will then start with a new bank and investment plan."

I shook my head. "This isn't exactly lawyer's work."

Again the smile. "Use your imagination."

"Well, what is at stake here, Mrs. Lundberg?"

"More than two million dollars."

Now I was paying careful attention. "Over the years has there been activity in these accounts?"

"My bank here, and I change banks often, arranges a draw down of money each year."

"For?"

"My support…and my daughter's. I take larger draws from time to time. Some is reinvested using brokerage accounts here."

"Is that your daughter with you?" I nodded toward the door.

The woman nodded yes, stood, put her hands on the desk and leaned toward me. I felt myself wanting to lean backward, or was it forward? This was one impressive lady. She had a low voice for the moment.

"Are you interested in my little matter, Mr. Brac? Will you take us on?"

"Us?"

"Astrid, my daughter and me. She is my guardian of sorts, but I don't burden her with my business affairs." She suppressed a laugh, "I'm very secretive."

"Yes, well, I consider myself engaged. We can get together again in person or by phone and discuss details."

"And your retainer?" She looked amused.

"That's not necessary. I will bill you monthly; my fee is $100 an hour. Is that agreeable?"

"Yes...yes, it is. I'm not interested in delaying things. Can we talk now?"

"Of course."

She sat back and dug in the large purse she was carrying. Out came several documents.

"Here is a list of my Swiss accounts with the access numbers. Actually, all of this is at the same bank." She floated it across my desk. Interesting reading; my rough tally put the balance at close to three million.

"You have more than you said." I gave her my sincere smile.

"I said around two million, that was accurate, was it not?" She gave me her sincere smile.

I confirmed to myself that this one was a tough and smart lady who might be a dangerous, demanding client. She was just too put together.

"Here's the Swiss form of Power of Attorney which will allow you to operate. We have to execute one of these at the Swiss counsel's office."

I nodded and said, "Okay, whenever it suits you."

"I'm hoping for today or tomorrow. Can you make the trip to Basel within a week or so?"

I felt pressure, trapped and uneasy. "Can I ask why the urgency?"

She took a deep breath. "It's just me, Mr. Brac, sometimes my thoughts start spinning. Fear takes over. I'm overwhelmed, I need to settle what's bothering me."

"Bringing this sum of money into the U.S. could trigger inquiries, from the tax authorities for instance."

"Let them inquire. The money is mine, legally earned and then invested. I am told my tax filings are correct."

I needed more. "Does your accountant know about your foreign-based assets?"

Here came the smile again. "My accountants know all about me."

I plowed on. "Can I speak with them?"

She was ready for this. A business card was pushed across the table. I glanced at it. Who the hell were "Honest & Semi, CPAs?

"Okay, you mentioned there are people who might want to talk with you about this. Did I get that right?"

"That part is history. You have no need to know, as they say. What I hope you will do is liquidate my Swiss holdings, get a cashier's check and bring it here. That's all."

I leaned back in my chair, stared at the ceiling and made the right decision, I hoped. My motivation was not a trip to Europe, it was the girl, Astrid, who had caught my fancy among other things. I straightened up and grabbed my calendar.

"I can go next Saturday. Do business on the following Monday."

Boy, did she have the smile working now. "That's wonderful, Mr. Brac, just wonderful. When you travel, please go first class."

"I always do."

We laughed together.

As I took her out of my office, we were each in our own way taken aback by the scene in the reception. Astrid, on full view, was simply an overwhelming young woman. She was laughing loudly at or with an older man who was seated facing her. He was talking vigorously using his hands and arms for emphasis.

He loudly said, "So I took charge and turned the bucket over and put it on his head. Of course, there was a bit remaining and it oozed down his face." He gave her a leer. The young woman cracked up.

I almost yelled, "Dad, this, uh…"

He boomed, "Sonny, this doll is perfect…Astrid, here he is, the victim minus the bucket of crap."

She gave me a look, still laughing…at me no doubt.

I mumbled, "Hello, I'm Sonny Brac," and to my new client I got out, "this is my father, an embarrassment at times."

"I'm sure he is," Anita jumped into the ring and introduced herself. Codfish took a hard look and seemed to falter a bit. He fixed on the moment and Anita. That was it. "I've met my match," Dad told himself…or so the story would go.

The trio left together. I could imagine the show the ladies got on their way out of the building. Mr. Funny, that being Dad, was front and center. That girl, Astrid, had to be followed up on - now.

That evening was a downer before it started. I told myself that I was not in the mood for my first date with Dede Figueroa. But as a normal, horny young man, I plotted my moves anyway. The business manager looked like she needed and wanted her business managed.

"Boy, is she loaded," was how I put it, at least to myself. We left the mag's office in a blur. Dede was wearing the outfit she favored for strutting her stuff around LIVE/DIE. Her uniform was a tight skirt and sweater, usually matching in color, and a single strand of pearls. Well, it was businesslike, but also a turn on. Dad noted more than once that the girl "was blessed."

"Is this a surprise party, Sonny, or do you know where we're going?" She could have been laughing at me.

I was driving slowly and glancing at her as often as possible. I was glancing at her chest if it must be known. I had told myself that I didn't even want to go on this date. Astrid was the one, this was a waste of time. How I lied. Lust had taken over.

"A restaurant, Dede, is our goal. Doros to be precise, know it?"

"I don't go out much, Sonny, and not to fancy restaurants anyway." She laid on a self-satisfied smile.

"How do you know Doros is fancy?" I could smile too.

"Sonny, I suspect you're a sophisticated guy. I watch you - very nice, expensive clothes, a big time car. You're suave, well-mannered. All the admirable traits a girl looks for."

Boy, was this laying it on. How to respond? My brain stalled for a few seconds.

"There's sophisticated or simple, Dede. I'm really a simple type. Say what I think. For example, I'd very much like to violate you, in a friendly way."

"You're beyond simple, you're a simpleton."

I drove up to the parking attendant and we took the necessary steps to get in the restaurant and wait our turn for the maitre d'. My date was silent. Perhaps I'd overshot the runway again.

At the table she rather calmly addressed me as I sort of hid behind my menu. "Sonny, you're still a sophisticated guy, even when you're rude. Or should I say crude? Anyway, I'm aware of your teenage urges. Most guys rush it, hope for a quick conquest or whatever you call it. I say, keep 'em suspended. Let the drooling bastards work for it. I never let it be known when or if I'm going to participate. Get it?"

Okay, I got it. I furled my colors. "God, I'm sorry, Dede. Your position is really the only one a woman should take, and I respect it."

Dede grinned, "Bullshit."

Dinner came and went and so did we. Her apartment, which was in one of those dumpy buildings on outer California Street became ground zero. Dede drew the line - at her waist.

"Sonny, that's it." She pushed me away. "It's a first date. For God's sake, I'm a graduate of Stanford."

I went limp and so did it.

Back in my apartment, my Astrid mania took over. That girl burned in my mind. That pursuit would come, but for the moment I savored the perfect rejoinder. To any request, demand or plea, just say, "No, I'm a graduate of Stanford."

I went to Basel armed with the power of attorney and a copy of the letter my client had sent to her bank explaining that she was closing her accounts. You always fear something is going to go wrong no matter how much documentation and whatever else you drag into a deal. I felt naked with only two pieces of paper and my good looks when I walked into Udderbanken. Not to worry, a polite gentleman only kept me waiting two days after he'd taken my paltry offering and disappeared behind a closed door.

His secretary was cordial, flirty and probably available. I wasn't. I spent my waiting time planning the Astrid campaign. Her mother was one tough broad, as Dad would say, like mother like daughter?

Finally the bank man called me at my hotel to report all assets had been converted to cash. The fees were handsome to say the least. I went by for the cashier's check, the banker's limp handshake and a come-on look from his secretary. One look at her and it was manifest that she worked at the right bank. I drank most of the way home.

CHAPTER 6

"I can't get no satisfaction."

"In what way, Dad?"

"This goddamn magazine is stalled in case you're missing your frontal lobe. I cleared the hopeless out; now we're thin on bodies, we need help. We need hitters to get this rag some circulation. Now!"

A typical Codfish rant. Of course it was largely self-indulgent…watching others scramble was sport. We had advertised and otherwise put the word out that LIVE/DIE was hiring. Resumes came, people dropped by but so far the talent pool did not contain Dad's kind of fish. The applicants for the editor slot were a dismal group which retreated, to a man, after an interview with the publisher.

Dad wanted a local guy. Yes, he said "guy." Connected but not attached (whatever that meant), fearless and on and on. I asked about preferred height and weight.

"Not funny, just go find him, fast." Codfish broke off to give the passing Dede a careful look.

After that, wouldn't you go for a drink? I did. Most of the regulars at the mid-afternoon call at Mooney's gave me a nod or a hello. I went to the end of the bar and pulled in next to a guy I'd met but didn't know.

He turned with a wan smile and reintroduced himself, "Hi, Roy Incisor."

"Sonny, Sonny Brac, how'ya doin?" I nodded to Sean who had delivered my usual. I checked out Roy as I had a few sips. He appeared somewhat loaded, a bit rocky and downcast. What you do with this situation is change stools or at least keep your mouth shut. Bars are full of depressed people, as if pouring down a depressant helps. Today I was trying hard to take care of Sonny and let others take care of themselves. So much for that.

Roy turned to me staring with his little red pig eyes. "I'm fucked up, sorry, bad company...I just lost my job."

"That's tough...where were you working?" He was staring at the back of the bar and trying to focus. Roy was a presentable, small man who was one of those guys who looked young but wasn't. He had stark white skin which allowed his veins, blood vessels or whatever to be clearly featured on his temples and hands. He gathered himself. "Do you have a few minutes?"

I nodded.

"You're the lawyer, right?"

"Yup."

"Your old man is the new owner of LIVE/DIE."

Again I acknowledged.

"Okay, well I might have a story for him. Naturally for a price."

"Naturally."

"I want a job, need a job. So that's it." He looked away. Probably because he was tearing up.

I tried to rescue the guy. "Well, that's between Dad and you. I'll hear you out for a couple of minutes but it'll get you precious little I suspect."

He gave me a dollar from a small stack of bills on the bar. "Keep it and I'll tell you. I paid you so the conversation is privileged."

I laughed. "That one has many holes, I'm not your lawyer, can't be, don't want to be. I have a conflict. You're nosing around to negotiate with my client; LIVE/DIE is my client."

Roy played with his stack of bills acting as if his head had cleared a bit. I ordered a second drink, offered him one and got a decline.

He turned, a ninety degree effort and faced me. "Okay, Sonny, I'll tell you…no strings. A request though. If you think this story is hot I want your help in getting to your old man, 'er father. I need a good word about a job. So you'll know, I've been at both papers and for the last few years the spokesman for the Endorsement League. Been around."

I nodded, and he went on. A nod is not a commitment, a lesson taught to me by several young ladies.

"You know anything about the League?"

"Not much," I replied…actually I knew nothing.

"The League is a not so subtle way to get candidates and propositions - ballot measures - to pay big time for an endorsement. It has a long standing reputation for bi-partisan analyses and voting recommendations. Its endorsements are important, prized in many races."

He sucked at the ice cubes in his empty glass. Naturally, I offered, "Want another?"

"Uh, okay."

I held up two fingers and before long fresh drinks were in front of us. Roy was not going to be stopped and he wasn't. He talked away.

Hot had been Roy's word. I would line up incredulous, outrageous and exploitable and add them to the mix. My companion's story was a scandal that would rock the town. The immediate future of LIVE/DIE could be looking up to say the least.

This was one of those times when the supreme commander had to be bothered. I knew that I had to hang on to Roy. He was loaded and talking, a volatile combination.

"I'll call my dad, let's see if we can connect."

"Now?"

"Why not - he's mellow in the late afternoon... sometimes."

In a few minutes we were in my car headed through North Beach and down Montgomery Street toward the magazine's office. My passenger put his head out the window to "get some air" and had a fine puke for the better part of a block.

Roy thought he'd pulled himself together, or so he told me. I put my usual warning regarding Dad on ice. It was a courtesy I extended when I brought a stranger to the throne. This time no...Roy had to sell his story and himself.

"My good man, you look like you need a drink." Dad was smiling.

Roy wasn't, he declined. I helped with a bit of background, Roy seemed somewhat frozen. Then he curiously straightened out and rapidly talked. He spoke clearly and almost eloquently as a rapt Codfish listened. The small man was nothing less than impressive as he told the sordid story. Dad kept biting his lip as Roy poured it on. This was a sure sign that he was an exhilarated Codfish. Hearing Roy's tale of evil for the second time cemented my belief this story could make LIVE/DIE.

Dad was on his feet as the disheveled man wound down. "Ever been an editor, Roy?" Codfish gave him the fish eye.

"Nice, Dad, of course he hasn't. You just heard his resume." That's what crossed my mind. Say it? No way.

"No, sir…but I've been around enough editors to know the drill. It's not an art, but it is a skill. You have to have command of the language, command of the troops and style. And, of course, you follow the message."

Dad went magnanimous, "That's it, well put. What about the publisher? How does he fit?"

"He's the Chairman Mao."

"You're hired, my dear man…Sonny will take care of the details. My magazine is about dirt, you're bringing some, now you'll have to get more. We expose everything but ourselves…unless asked."

I patted myself on the back for finding an editor. It was a start but only that. The magazine was still so shaky it was like a bad hangover. We had no writers, no in-house talent. Roy's little number would have to be farmed outside and that posed problems galore. "But having an editor means measurable progress," I told myself.

* * * * *

My heavy thinking often took place at Mooney's. Usually I could hide and drink in peace during the day. On a certain late afternoon as I was doing myself wrong, Dad was prowling elsewhere. Had I known the details I would have soiled myself.

Codfish felt a tinge of nerves; he rang the bell and put on a best boy smile for the maid who answered, "May I help you, sir?"

"May I please see Mrs. Lundberg?"

"Whom may I say is calling?"

"Mr. Brac."

"Thank you, please come in."

He waited in the entry, pulled at his collar and then fooled with the unaccustomed tie.

"Please come this way."

The large man was led to a well-appointed room with a sensational bay view. But that's not where he looked.

"Mr. Brac, this is a surprise. Am I in trouble or something?"

"No, no, of course not, please call me Codfish, I have some trouble myself."

She suppressed a smile. "I see, won't you sit down."

The maid reappeared and offered them iced tea.

"What's your trouble, if I can be so direct, Mr. Brac."

"Well, I have trouble figuring out how to court." Codfish grinned, "I'm here to court you."

"How does one court these days?" she coolly asked. Anita was dressed in slacks, a loose top, and low-heeled sandals. Her face was as perfect as lineage and make-up could create.

"Well, I think you court in person. I mean to start with. I'm here because I have you on my mind - have had since we met in Sonny's office. You're a beautiful woman and I'm taken with you." He had shifted to a serious demeanor, at least for Codfish.

"That's it?" She raised her eyebrows and shook her head.

"There's more, you can find out if you wish."

The woman shifted in her chair, thought for a few seconds and then spoke, "Courting has to go on for a while. The parties get to know each other - know if they like each other. You do understand that, don't you, Mr. Brac?"

"Codfish, please. Do you have a problem with Codfish?"

"No, if that's your name. But I prefer something else if it's available." Again the raised eyebrows.

"Call me W.T. if you wish." He forced a smile. The Codfish brain was spinning, "Jesus Christ, all this over my name, I'll be dead before I get to first base with her."

"W.T., then, that wasn't so hard, was it? In Scandinavia some men call their thing their cod. So I'm protecting you somewhat. She took her glass of iced tea to her mouth and looked at him with dancing eyes.

"Okay, Anita, you win, W.T. is officially courting you...let's go to dinner."

"And why not?" she thought.

He liked Hal's, a small steakhouse on Powell right by the cable car turnaround. They were given a secluded table; he wanted booze - scotch; she asked for Dubonnet.

Determined, that was it; both were as things evolved. The approach might have been careful, but before too long they let loose. He slurped his drink and it was quickly gone. Codfish, W.T. now, signaled for another. She shook her head. He started humming; Anita guarded, mumbled, "Do I bore you?"

"Huh? God, no."

"But you are singing."

"Humming is a life long habit when I'm nervous."

"Oh, dear, and what's your private song?"

He blurted, "Seven Years With the Wrong Woman."

"What?"

"Never mind. All this will take time."

"All what?"

"Our life stories, so to speak, you know, instant acquaintanceship or something. Jesus!"

Anita smiled, "I'll tell you all - maybe, please relax. Drink some more and forget worrying. And stop saying 'Jesus.'"

"Yes, yes, I'm sorry. Shit. Okay, here's the deal. I saw you and that was it. This happened only once before. That was when I first collided with my deceased wife." He had a pleading look that appeared quite genuine.

"All right, I could like you, too, but I am a conservative, cautious and conniving woman. What do you want? Sooner or later I'll have to know. Sooner is preferred." She gave him a dazzling smile and went on, "Men usually want sex and that's fine with me, even at my age. But I decide, the man doesn't."

He nodded, looked at her and said, "Of course, I'm not a pusher, I can wait."

"I'll bet."

Codfish plunged on. "You're right. Why screw around? What do I want? I think I want you in every possible way. I'm getting murdered, I need to relax." He shrugged his shoulders and took a heavy hit from his scotch.

"You've enjoyed your share of women, right, W.T.?"

This was a conservative? "Well, okay, hell, yes. Lots. I don't know how many."

"I'll guess they were all younger than you."

"Probably." He wondered, "Now what? It's like dating a shrink. All veils and puzzles. Ca-ca."

"And your age is?"

"Fifty-four."

"I'm sixty years old."

"Balls, I don't believe it."

"I'm not joking, it's the sad truth."

"Well, Anita, you look younger than I do and you move better."

She fired back, "If I look younger it's because you've mistreated yourself with alcohol and young girls. That could be why you look a bit older than you are." She smiled, not a kind smile, he thought.

He rubbed his face, "That kinda hurts, hell, I'm robust, rugged looking. Jesus." He looked at her and read nothing. "Age doesn't matter, you're as old as you feel. I feel young, why, because I'm with you."

"You mean because I'm older."

"Hell no," he hit the table with the palm of his hand. Place settings jumped and so did a few patrons, heads turned. Codfish was a closer, and now he tried, "You are a great broad, looks, smarts, self-containment. You're the complete package. You know it, I know it. Let's move on."

She was enjoying his torture and her expression didn't hide it.

They ordered their steaks and sides. Codfish consumed another scotch, she passed, and he ordered a bottle of cabernet franc, his usual.

She said, "I guess I will answer your unasked questions. Yes, every part of my body works," she paused, "every part. I have been known to enjoy sex."

"I really wasn't into that."

"Don't lie - you're not that drunk, are you?"

"This could turn into combat," thought the Codfish, time for a Neville Chamberlain. "Come on, Anita," he slurred a bit, "I'm in your hands - you have a sexy accent, that goes with the rest," he paused, "you know."

"I'm sorry I forgot to mention that I'm a bit of a bitch. A bitch with an accent. I'm beginning to like you, W.T., don't be so cowering." He covered his face with his hands.

"I'm a terribly difficult aging woman. I've given up on men for a combination of reasons. It's really a transition from functioning to what? Old age semi-functioning, I can't say. You are a darling to put up with me."

There was the opening. "If you're the glorious broad you appear to be we're going on. You won't believe it." His stare confirmed his words.

"I'm insecure, afraid at times, and somewhat lonely. You have the advantage, you see, don't abuse it." She stared right back at him.

"No way, sweetheart."

"Look," she shoved her hands toward him. They rested just north of his plate and the untouched steak.

"Yeh, so'?"

"They are wrinkled, spotted, and old appearing. Always look at the hands, it's an infallible guide. My hands are old. My face is a younger woman's. So is most of the rest of me. But old age terrifies me. The hands have gone, perhaps the rest of me will soon follow."

"Okay, that's a natural fear. But I don't care when or if you wrinkle. You should see the cod. He, at rest, is a wrinkled baby.

"Don't be vulgar. Will I have to say that often to you?" She raised her eyebrows.

"Popeye sez, 'I yam what I yam.' It's too late to change."

"Your poor wife must have suffered so."

"Yes, ma'am, in many ways, but I really broadened her vocabulary." He smiled and plowed into his cooling steak.

Anita excused herself. Not a bite, he noted. As she walked away his eyes followed her. She was so erect, a smooth walker, great ass, too.

He ate, waited, drank, waited. "What the hell?" When she returned he couldn't get a read from her expression. Anita slipped into her chair with a slight smile, "Sorry."

Codfish did not give her a pass. "So, what happened? Are you okay?"

"Yes, I'm out of practice. Uncoordinated. Embarrassed. I was trying to get my diaphragm in." She buried him with her look.

"What, I mean…"

"Are you that far gone? I can joke too."

"Jesus, you got me."

The woman tossed her red hair and attacked her cold food.

At her door, she folded into his embrace. They kissed, just like kids, he mused, and then she took over.

"Not tonight, Mr. Brac. It is not right for me yet. You don't understand, how can you? You're a man."

Codfish thought he had caught, weighed and put this one in the box. Holy shit. "Why?"

"Just because I'm not playing. But I do want you to come back."

"I see." He was too loud.

"No, you don't. Please call me soon. Goodnight, Mr. W.T. Codfish Brac." She kissed him.

He reached and accidentally placed his hand on her left one. She let it lie and he was instantly moved. After a moment she broke away, turned and went into her flat.

Codfish felt screwed on the one hand and happy on the other. The other being the hand still tingling from the feel of her tit. "Man, she's got 'em."

In his car, the man had a few thoughts. "I'm going to call my shrink, my doctor, Sonny - anybody. This reminds me of the time I fell in love with that scientist. She was so goddamn smart my brain had blisters just trying to keep up. No shit, this is it. Guys like me are always chasing the young stuff. Fun enough, mostly in the sack. The girls are just that...girls. They try too hard. Intelligent ain't smart. And how many intelligent little ladies have I met anyway? Hell, it's just the after game. They're after me for my money, and I'm after them for their honey."

He laughed out loud, squealed the Lotus away from a stop sign and refocused. "Now, an older woman, who'd think of it. Old playboy chases old skirt. The world is upside down. Hello Madagascar."

CHAPTER 7

Dede Figueroa announced the meeting, noting that Mr. Brac had suggested unanimous attendance. It was a transparent message; this was an event not to be avoided. Actually it was billed as a social hour, "Meet and Greet Our Gang." At the appointed time the conference room rapidly filled with the summoned. Worthy Feckheimer brought his artistic self. Lurking in the corner was Wally Moundminer, Mr. Food & Beverage, now Mr. On-The-Hit-List. The blow to Bergen Bode's back had not been forgotten by either Brac. Codfish allowed that he was "still mad enough to piss thumbtacks." Sonny and Dede made up the rest of the roster for the moment.

The publisher came in with his secretary, Barbara Boring, a half step behind him. Was she patting his ass? So it appeared. He had his sly look in play.

"Let's sit down," ordered Codfish. He looked to Dede, "Who's missing? Somebody's not here."

"Roy is waiting."

"Yes, Roy is waiting. Anybody know why?"

There were headshakes and an odd look passed between Wally and Worthy; there was a distinct odor of fear in the air. Codfish roared, "Shit, I know your lame thinking. He's still employed. In fact he's a genius, old Roy brought in a two-fer."

"A two-fer?" mumbled Wally.

"*Si*, two for one. We have two new reporters, writers, whatever. They are twins and inseparable, I'm told. No, not Siamese, Sonny."

On occasion Dad liked to use me to make a point. He continued, "Yes, our ace investigative reporters are identical twins and now before you meet them you can read an example of their work."

Barbara started passing a small stack of papers around the table. Dad said, "This piece is more human interest, or something, but I want you to absorb the style, the writing style. This is a masterpiece."

I took the handout, a couple of stapled pages, and started to read.

"Olympian Pet Tragedies, Pet Courage - 1984"
By (this part was blanked out)

"Television coverage of the L.A. Olympics brought viewers a dull collection of insipid stories about the personal lives of athletes. While these less than compelling vignettes were stupidly interrupted from time to time by coverage of athletic events, their impact lingers. Strangely, and for unknown reasons, the stories of athletes and their pet tragedies and their pet courage were flatly ignored.

There are countless inspirational yarns which could have been reported. The following is but a small sample of what was denied to viewers and covered up. Yes, we say covered up!

Take Cosmo Lecken, the one-armed archer from Liechtenstein. His dexterity was just short of fabulous even though he finished last. What wasn't told was the fact that Cosmo's arm was lost in a pet tragedy. Mr. Lecken was given a baby lion by his doting parents. The lion, named Leo, one day bit off his master's arm. The brave guy overcame this tragedy to become an Olympic archer. Leo was forgiven for his natural tendencies and still lives with the athlete. Olympians and their pets!

It is unsettling to think of the twin pet tragedies of Mike and Ike Bladder of Walla Walla, Washington. These lads, who are identical twins, also married identical twins, Maureen and Eileen Over. The foursome met when each of them adopted a dog from the same litter! Without warning Maureen and Eileen left Mike and Ike and took all the dogs with them. This horrible pet tragedy did not stop these tough men from becoming volunteer bus drivers at the LA Olympics. As a small but key cog in the transportation system, the Bladders somehow drove their buses, full of athletes, all the way to Tijuana, Mexico. Boy, were they popular! Olympic spirit, Olympic workers, and a pet tragedy forgotten as it rained margaritas for days.

Who else would be from Michigan but Bobbie Detroit? Ms. Detroit set an Olympic record for the 420 meter side-stroke. Her "surprise" for the rabid fans was her pet wolverine! Yes, indeed, she brought the snarling rascal to the Olympic medal ceremonies! Due to a series of blunders on the part of Olympic officials, the pet got loose and raised holy hell with the audience. Numerous bites and scratches later, the wily animal escaped. Accordingly, no more live pets will be allowed at medal ceremonies in any Olympic venue! It takes a tragedy.

Moral and Oral Responsibility, friends call them "Clean and Jerk," are weight lifters out of Shrimp Corner, Wyoming. You want gerbils? The brothers kept and nurtured over two hundred of the furry little darlings. Each beast had a name as did their large home room. The latter was fondly called "Poop House." The brothers returned from the gym one day to find their house filled with gas, of the natural variety. Their parents and siblings were gone - literally - but not the gerbils. The clever beasts had apparently escaped through a cracked window. When men cry it can be devastating. When male weight lifters cry a lot of image goes down the tube. But not to worry, Clean and Jerk dedicated their lifting to their lost gerbils. As a result, the missing critters made Olympic competitors out of two morons. Isn't that what it's all about?

One of the other athletes to bring a pet to Los Angeles was the Mexican high jumper, Rosa Sucor. This girl, only eleven years old, had been jumping since before she was walking. Her inspiration? Escaping her uncle and love of her pet chicken, Nafta. The bird was at her peck and call and accompanied the little soarer to all track meets. Rosa swore she couldn't jump if Nafta wasn't there.

In L.A., in one of those fiascos that only the Olympic Committee could produce, Nafta was rounded up as Rosa slept. The purpose? Random drug testing, so they said. Well, a missing bird, a distressed Rosa, and a fat lie from Olympic poobah, Dick Warmer, "We are turning the village inside down; we'll find Nafta." He should have looked in that night's fried chicken. An Olympic Pet Tragedy to say the least. Rosa had dreams and visions for a couple of days. She heard her chicken clearly say, "You didn't eat the chicken; that's good, I had worms. Keep your beak and cheeks closed, you'll win."

Rosa took gold (her roommate's jewelry) but failed to place in the competition. What might have been? Rosa was given a lovely stuffed toy chicken by the U.S. Women's Gymnastic Team.

A final, compelling vignette involves the executive secretary of the Olympic Committee, Antonio Juanito. Unbeknownst to many, Sr. Juanito kept his keys to everything Olympic on his person. His key chain was firmly attached his good luck charm, a live rat. The rat spent the entire Olympics in Mr. Juanito's pocket and apparently is none the worse for it. However, one way to put it is that Mr. Juanito has a "pocketful of miracles" as a result.

Tragedy, athletic courage, pet courage. Why didn't television let us know?"

People stopped reading, exchanged smiles, quizzical looks and chuckles. I was the only one that spoke, "Jeez, whoever wrote this crap is really twisted."
Barbara handed Dad a baton or a wand or something of the kind which he waved vigorously while shouting, "Great Spirit, give us twins."
She did.
Through the conference room door came Roy with a blond on each arm. The identical twins were short and round with angelic faces. Each little man seemed to move in several directions at the same time.

Roy, with a straight face, fired away. "May I present our new team. Our investigative team. You're meeting two ace reporters who have sterling reputations. Here's one example, they broke the Houston oil, sewage, and sex scandal. On my right is Juan Lawn and on my left John Lawn."

The twins took a bow - simultaneously.

My impression was, first this was not a joke and second, LIVE/DIE was about to follow the second word on its masthead.

Codfish took over. "I've spent a few minutes with the Lawn brothers and I'm impressed with their description of how they work. What's the word? Clever or dirty? Anyway, they get the stuff. Want to say a word, gents?"

The blond heads, together, shook a no.

"Okay, next item on the vagina," Dad said, reading from what looked like a piece of parchment. "We will address loyalty, secrecy and lunch, maybe in that order. To stick with LIVE/DIE you have to sign a loyalty and secrecy pact. Right now. Why? We are launched on a crusade and the Lawns are leading the way. There can be no leaks about what we're doing. You can sign or leave. The rest of our employees will be given the same option this afternoon. Take it away, Sonny!" he bellowed and madly waved his wand.

"This form is usual, industry standard, in fact it is based on one used by a fellow publisher," I lied.

Dad lied too. "That's Melwert Confit of In and Out Your Window."

This got a smile, in tandem, from the Lawns.

I continued. "Note the penalty clause, Number twenty-nine. If you breach this you are subject to immediate discharge and legal hell."

The forms were passed around. Pens flew into action.

Codfish was leaning back in his chair, eyes half closed - "Everybody sign?"

I had the forms once again, "Yes, sir."

"Okay, here's the story."

The Lawns gave a collective throat clear. Juan or John spoke with a pronounced lisp. "Yeth, we invethtigate - anything, anybody. Then we write about it. Then we run like hell when it's publithed."

The twins chuckled, in unison.

"Here in Frithco you got a rotten meth in the Congrethional race. The fix is in, we thuspect. Why? Because thomebody told us, and we believe him." Roy, the somebody just mentioned, had on his poker face.

There was simultaneous vigorous nodding of their bowling ball heads. "You want to know how it'th going to be fixed - who's doing it? Tho do we! We'll find the evil, we'll bore out the tunnelth of crookedneth, we'll kick thom asseths."

The brothers concluded by shaking hands, then they embraced. Their audience sat silently.

Codfish stood up, put his hands on the table and softly said, "You two clowns are going to make thith magazine."

The meeting adjourned and oddly Codfish asked me for a ride.

"Lose your car, Dad?"

"Not exactly. Take me up to the St. Francis. I am having tea with Mrs. Lundberg."

"Tea you say?"

"Tea, I say."

I didn't press - let the old lech do it his way. Traffic held us up and Dad was agitated. "Shit, why'd you go up Geary? This is a crawl."

"It's not my doing - these fucking cars. This is the best way usually."

"Not today. I don't want to be late. This woman is something else, I'm on best behavior and that means on time."

I took the plunge. "How's she something else?"

"I mean she's attractive." He gave me the fish eye. "And I mean really attractive."

We sat in silence as the stop and go traffic edged on.

Dad popped the question he must have been saving for this kind of occasion, "Are you her lawyer now?"

"Yes, everything is privileged, you know it. Don't ask."

He growled, "Oh, I know, counselor, proctor, whatever the fuck you call yourself." He gave me a hard look which meant "just kidding." He added, "What are her measurements?"

I dropped the smitten Codfish and drove over to Harrington's, a great bar in an awful neighborhood. I waded through a gang of less fortunates who decorated the sidewalk and made it into the dark interior. A few day drinkers took up stools and a couple of tables. I needed isolation so I took my gin and tonic to a booth. Now I would sort it out.

And what was there to sort? Hell, life looked okay - the magazine, my practice, my new client, her daughter. Well, that was it, wasn't it? That incredible girl. A chance meeting, just a quick moment when I took her mother into my office. Then as she left there was Dad bullshitting the glorious thing. I had no chance. I'd been clobbered by an angel, that was it. I was sober, dead so, it was not an illusion, she wasn't anything but splendid. I'd been circling the truth ever since I saw her. I told myself, "Time to take charge, old boy. Shape up, time waits for nobody." Gin is so helpful.

This private review and analysis took a couple of drinks. I drove back to my office - carefully. There was a message or two - Mrs. Lundberg had called at noon. I returned the call, no answer. She was with Dad, I knew, but I was hoping for a contact with Astrid.

Coffee, fooling with mail, and fifteen minutes burned. I tried Mrs. Lundberg again. An answer, a female, the glorious daughter perhaps.

"Hello, this is Sonny Brac. I'm assuming Astrid. I'm returning your mother's call."

"I'm sorry my mother is having her teeth pulled."

"Huh? Is this the Lundberg residence?"

"It is."

"Okay, is this Astrid?"

"It is."

"Are you giving me a bad time?"

"Yes." Then she laughed. "I'm told I have no sense of humor, no gaiety. I'm so," she drew it out, "serious."

"I like jokes, even if they're on me." Where should I go? "Anyway, your mother is not available I take it." I waited.

"A reply occurred to me...I'll skip it. She's out with somebody."

"Can, ah, do you - are you interested in dinner tonight - this is a late invitation, but..."

"You mean with you?"

I could read her smile over Ma Bell's wire. "Yes, of course, with me."

"Why not - I'm hungry - you're whatever. It has to be early. I go to bed early, get up early."

"Sure, I'll pick you up at Union Street, say six. What's your pleasure?"

"You'll never know. But I like simple places, simple food and simple conversation." It came in a short, quick burst. She sounded like she was reading from a cue card.

I took her to Ernies. What's wrong with red-flocked walls, white on white tables, great service and faux French food? Astrid was unimpressed and she told me so rather directly.

I tried a lawyer-like answer. "Yes, of course I heard your request for simple. This is kind of simple, I think. Maybe not. Yes, I respect your wishes. Yes, we're underdressed. Yes, I'm known here. That's not why I'm tolerated. I'm tolerated because I pay these outrageous prices without a whimper."

She had nodded her way through my admission. Now it came, the second wave that is.

"Sonny, you need to study women from afar. We are not orchids - fragile, look but don't touch. We're a match for men, and we're not just for coupling. You are nice, handsome I guess, and a half-hearted little hustler."

My face fell. I could feel it.

She pulled back. "I'm sorry, bad words and bad me. What I mean is you're a project, the results could be fine. I sound horrible. But, look at you drink, look at your eyes - Jesus, Sonny."

"What?" I took a sip or rather a slurp of my drink. "I mean, hell, Astrid, are you a doctor or something?"

Nobody told me - I was afraid to ask her mother, my client, about her lovely daughter. So when it came it almost laid me out.

"Yes, I'm a doctor. I work in the emergency room at UCSF. My residency was there. Now I'm on staff." She looked up at me and then down at her salad. Her quick look at my face must have been enough to record my amazement.

"Congratulations," I mumbled. To drink or eat I wondered. I ate.

As we struggled on, it wasn't a productive conversation. I asked about doctoring and she spouted. That was it. The doctor had no further questions of me. Astrid had scared the shit out of me and to prove it, I had abstained from further drink for the remainder of the hurried meal.

It was a quiet, make that morbid, ride home. I double parked on Union Street and started to get out of the car. My arm was tugged and I settled back.

"I can get in Sonny. Thank you for dinner. This is not a lost cause unless you want it to be." She leaned over and kissed my lips. She lingered a few seconds and then got out of the car without looking back.

I started making self-improvement promises as I drove to my apartment. Hell, nothing like Astrid had ever come my way and I felt smart enough to go for the gold when I had the chance. I would start tomorrow.

* * * * *

Congressman Gavin Mummiform died of a heart attack as he walked across the lobby of his bank. The venerable lawmaker had just deposited a large sum of cash consisting of gifts from constituents, lobbyists, and the Republic of China. His death was a huge loss for San Francisco as the quiet little man did bring home the bacon. His signature phrase, said over and over was simply, "If it's good for San Francisco, then it's great for me."

A special election to fill the empty Congressional seat was called and a miserable, mean cat fight took place as the parties scrambled to select their candidates. The smelly back stabbing spawned Bob O. Shine for the G.O.P. and Gunther S.S. Geil for the Democrats.

The campaign, for a March special election, would get into full gear after the holidays. But well before the New Year, things became tawdry and dirty. Neither candidate discussed any issues beyond motherhood and family. They were in agreement on these critical concerns. Moms were wonderful and families just fine. Each candidate proudly claimed to have a mother.

The city was overwhelmingly Democratic; even a simpleton like Geil should win going away. Accordingly, few normal people paid attention or wasted time with the barnyard antics of the campaign.

But the pols had things to do. Evil things as usual. B. Overland Nicely went himself. He had ten thousand in cash and a .45, Army issue, loaded. The gun gave him solace...he'd used it in Korea and stopped the bastard cold. That was one of those "friendly fire" incidents. The "bastard" was his captain.

The meeting took place at a bar for the unnaturals, as B.O. charmingly put it, out on Polk Street. The guy, or whatever, was wearing a woman's hat with a lowered veil. A gloved hand motioned the chairman to sit. Nothing was said. The strange one pushed a large envelope across the table.

"If it's not talking neither am I," thought B.O.

He took the envelope, opened the clasp, raised the flap and pulled out three photos. All he needed was a quick look. He shoved the pictures back in, closed the envelope and took the bundled but not disguised money from his pocket and reached for the gloved hand. And it was over; and it was quick. B.O., a bit shaken, was out on the street into a cab in less than ten minutes after his arrival at the fetid bar. Now for the next step.

The GOP chairman was unhappy with meetings in bars; after all, he didn't drink and didn't approve of drinking. He had stopped using spirits years ago. It was a courageous act, so he thought, undertaken to support his alcoholic wife. They stayed dry together... for a while. Mrs. Nicely, sober after several cloudy years, got a good look at B.O. Need one say more? He was deeply hurt when she left. He remained ready to shoot on sight the abuse counselor that had stolen his wife away.

The sad man turned to his long-time love and shelter, the Republican Party. B.O. became a fixture as chairman. He knew how to get results, how to be ruthless, how to fight from a hopeless minority position and how to buzz the appropriate asses. He was as effective as a toll-taker's hand.

The chairman sat in a booth at the insider's saloon, Reno's, the only customer on a slow afternoon. He nursed a tall ginger ale and contemplated his friend's reaction. This would be sweet.

Topper Bello, dressed like Hopalong Cassidy, slid into the booth. Old Topper loved costumes. Off went his large cowboy hat and as he struggled to put it down he yelled an order for scotch and soda. The Demo chairman was known at Reno's, as well as dozens of other bars where he was smiled at and behind his back called a mark. He did tip well.

B.O. didn't wait. "Topper, the League endorsement has to go to B.O."

"What the fuck do you mean?"

"Not me, not this B.O. I mean B.O. Sinc; Bob O. Sinc. - our candidate."

Topper had his drink which he drained to the halfway mark. "Over my stiff weenie, you Republicans have too many B.O.s, it smells." He laughed.

But B.O. came back; he'd had a bad start. "Topper, let me lay it all out. Our candidate, Bob O., is going to be your next congressman. He easily wins the special election. Why? Because Gunther S.S. Geil is a pervert, a sick man. He makes me puke. I have, not we have, I have evidence that will destroy the fucking creep. I'll show you sometime...that sometimes is when you're on board - locked in." He paused, his eyes were shining brown marbles.

"Locked into what?" Topper hissed.

"Why the program, Topper, the program. I tell you, it's the only way for you. If you try to exit you're still trapped to remain silent. Why? Because I've got the ammo to destroy your sleaze and soon you will know all about it. Will you rat on him? I think not. Will you join me? I think so. Anyway, what you can do is help by keeping silent while I arrange the League's endorsement for Bob O. I am calling in all my chits, as they say. I'll get the votes, some on principle, some because they are a reward and some because some of our dear colleagues will be blackmailed. You will do nothing because you assume Gunther S.S. is going to win. It's in the bag, he's a shoo-in. Well, when we, the respected co-chairmen, announce the League's endorsement of B.O. you can express your surprise and amazement at the margin of victory for the underdog. My guess is that will be the first hot poker up your boy's ass."

117

"Cute." Topper didn't hide his anger. "All this is a fairy tale - are you back on the booze?"

"Cute…no. Don't get personal, Hoppy, I'm merely playing pin the bomb on the donkey. You're either in or out…now."

Topper was pissed. "What exactly do you think you have on Gunther? You gave me your lurid opinion, how about some evidence."

"I won't fool around." B.O. placed a large manila envelope on the table. "Hold your nose and take a look, Topper."

The grizzled Democrat, nervous and showing it, took the plunge. He looked. He shook his head, over and over again. "Christ, if they're real, I mean it's disgusting, horrible…he'll have to withdraw."

"No, he'll have to stay until these pictures appear a week or so ahead of the election."

"I won't go along with this shit - it's blackmail or worse. B.O., you're a sewer."

"Please, no personal asides. You'll go along, Topper, just the way you always do. It's fifty grand deposited in your bank account tomorrow." He raised his eyebrows and smiled.

Topper said nothing and signaled for another drink. He reviewed the prospects. Christ, a Republican congressman. There goes the lifeline or the money line, rather. He would be Mr. Outsider, no deals, no juice, no *nada*. He'd better take care of himself now.

"Okay, B.O., it will hurt my future income badly, you know that. I'll need one hundred."

"Seventy-five."

Topper nodded, "Seventy-five, that's the number."

B.O. reached across the table and grabbed Topper's limp hand. "You're a great American, Topper. Now the messy details. After the League endorses B.O. you have to start and support rumors about a weird Gunther. Nothing specific, just stuff like, 'There's something wrong with that guy, I can't put my finger on it,' and so on. Get some help from your friends. When the ball drops you will do everything in your power to crucify your candidate. There will be no legal way for a substitute candidate at that point. Even if Gunther quits, he's still on the ballot. You will find yourself reluctantly endorsing B.O. Sinc, it's a matter of decency."

Topper shook his head - he'd drained his drink and signaled for another. It quickly appeared and he started on it. "I can't do that. I can't endorse your cretin. Jesus, I'd be run out of town."

"Well, we will want you to keep your position as Demo chair, that's for sure. This won't be the only time we'll work together. The future is glorious, so, perhaps you're right, don't endorse Bob O., just trash your pervert. You will do that, right'?"

His companion felt the booze fuel rebellion. This was just plain crap, evil crap. The only thing that kept him here was the money. He would be in clover. "Yes, I can do that. I will do that. It's the only decent thing to do."

B.O. Nicely broke into an insincere smile. "Yes, my friend, you are Mr. Decent and I'm proud to know and work with you."

119

"Fuck you," Topper growled, "I'm me and I'll sleep well at night. After seeing those disgusting pictures I know Gunther has to be dumped...it's a matter of honor, the flag and our children."

"Yes, Topper, yes, indeed. Well, I'm on my way... God bless." B.O. slid out of the booth, laid a smug grin on Topper and headed for the street.

The suddenly terrified Democratic chairman stayed at Reno's. A few more scotches and he'd almost buried reality. His thought pattern consisted of fear and depression. This was too awful, for even the veteran politician had a modest conscience. Topper felt himself bleeding, he'd lost it all. Nothing was left but the money. Sure he knew the word, "quisling."

The sell-out walked slowly toward the League offices. He had to avoid Democratic headquarters. "Christ, would they see it on my face?"

Roy Incisor was on his way out of League headquarters with a box full of junk he'd left behind. Roy had stayed away after he had walked the plank during the last election. He had rejoiced as the voters trounced Prop. Q and celebrated by going on a toot for several days. When he was sober enough to talk he called both B.O. and Topper. The plea was the same, he needed work. Each pol was politely evasive.

Roy took a quick look at Topper as the wasted cowboy stumbled into headquarters. What was that outfit? "Topper, you out celebrating or what?"

"Get me a scottie, Roy, if you please, I've had a bit of a scare if you must know. Peckerneck stew, with bells and whistles." The man weaved toward a chair and then managed a sloppy landing.

The former press secretary went to the not so secret stash and poured a tumbler half full of whiskey.

"That's it - thanks, dear Roy." Topper slurred.

"So what, Topper, what can I do? You don't look yourself." Roy had seen the guy loaded before but this was different. The co-chairman's face and neck were grey. Battleship grey.

"It's nothing for you, Roy," Topper mumbled. Already the glass of scotch was nearly empty. "No, nothing. You stay away, forget it."

"Forget what? What's going on?"

"You promise to stay away?" Topper seemed to be pleading.

"Sure, yes," Roy was emphatic.

"Well, they're going to steal the congressional."

"What? Who is?"

"Never mind, stay away. Save yourself, it's just fucking horrible...election fraud, blackmail, perverts, you name it." The old man started to cry. After a moment, Topper struggled to his feet and took a few unsteady steps toward the door. He turned and in a loud whisper told Roy, "This never happened, you never heard a word from me, right?"

"Sure, right."

Topper suddenly appeared modestly sober; he was ready to pronounce and he did. "You need a job, Roy, right?"

"Hell, yes."

"For your own good, young man, you won't need what's coming down. Stay out of politics, the League. I'll try to help you."

"Okay, Topper, I'm flying blind but you've usually been straight with me."

Topper mumbled a few words and lurched out the door. Roy processed or tried to process the information that had flowed from the drunken Democratic chairman. It had to be true, at least part of it. Surely he'd picked up enough to get somebody interested. Roy suddenly had something to play with. He so wanted to be a player.

CHAPTER 8

I couldn't take my eyes off of them. I tried not to stare, but what the hell, when I looked away my gaze rapidly wandered back to the preposterous twins.

There's a small couch among the furnishings in my office. It's more of a love seat, a decorative little number meant for one adult or two kids. Well, drop that theory. Both Lawns fit on the couch and they looked quite comfortable. The brothers were resplendid in white suits, white shirts, and off-white neckties. I was drawn to the sheer white stockings and two-tone black and white shoes. The outfits were modestly accessorize; each lad carried a white patent leather purse of sorts.

The Lawns had requested the meeting - I had no clue why. These days I seemed to genuinely have no clue about anything. Hooked on Astrid was my problem.

John, or Juan, opened. "Mr. Brac, Sr., hath requcthed that we now report to you. Thath why we're here."

"He forgot to tell me," I mused.

"He may be preoccupied." The twins exchanged a knowing glance. Were they going to titter? It looked like it.

One said, "We dig, find and expose." They both nodded vigorously. The other one, Christ, it was too embarrassing to ask names so they remained individually unidentified, took the stage. It should be noted that I'm sure that both twins lisped on occasion. They probably took turns.

"First, Sonny, Mr. Codfish put you in our loop not too many days ago."

"Really?"

"Yes, we were having tea, my brother and I, at the St. Francis and who should we encounter but your father. He was accompanied by an extremely handsome woman."

Here came the echo, "Extremely handthome."

"Mr. Brac made a delightful fuss," John/Juan looked at his twin for confirmation and he got it, "delightful futh." They nodded to each other. "He wanted a table for four so we could join them. It was just impossible; there's such a crowd at tea time."

"Okay, I'm listening." I tried to sound like someone who's in charge.

The other one took over. "Your father has a way about him. He's tho mathculine."

Now his brother chimed in, "In a nice way…a very nice way. Well, to be precise, money changed hands and we soon were seated together. The woman, introduced as Mrs. Lundberg, was polite but remote. Mr. Codfish, it was at this point we were instructed to call him Codfish, saw her agitation and suggested that they leave. She laughed and then spoke softly, 'Not after what you paid for this table. I'll be around the corner at Blums, I'm suddenly hungry, W.T.'"

"Mr. Codfish growled, "This won't take long, I'll get you."

"The lady left and Codfish signaled to the waiter. 'You boys want a drink? Drinking tea only goes so far.'

"We had mother's helpers. Codfish was direct." Now it was the other one speaking, "Quite direct."

"What was the result, what have you got?" I was obviously not controlling this agenda.

"Codfith had a thtare that pierced."

"A piercing stare."

I tried to move things, "And…?" This was followed with my version of Dad's piercing stare.

"And, we told him of our investigation to date. He said, I'll never forget, 'Holy fucking thit - take thith to Thonny once you tie up the looth endth. This will thell magazines galore and ruin a few liveth too.'"

I was near the end of feigned calmness, "Tell me, gents, tell me what you've got."

"Yes, thir, Thonny, we must report in chronological order."

"Please do that." I was so anxious I could have grabbed a throat or two.

"We checked out the mag's thaff. You know, who are we working with, who can be truthted, who can we uthe."

Here came the other one. "We chose Wally, Wally Moundminer. He's oblique, hard to ID, but we know, a woman in man's clothing. That's a phrase, you know. Wally wanted to help us, what we needed was a road map, a list of hangouts where gay folks talk politics first and the rest of it second. Your Food & Beverage editor was most helpful."

"Oh, for Christ's sake," was my immediate thought. "Here's the guy Dad wanted to maim because of what he did to Bergen and now he's been recruited by the Lawns. This has to be settled."

The other one took over. "Why did we thart this way? There are no more hip or knowledgeable people than that crowd. Politicth is an avocation for the gay community. We theek information from the informed. It workth."

The other Lawn was off the couch in a full performance mode, he moon walked and sort of sang. "We have an enormous expense account for a reason. Not self-help nor self-abuse. No, we spend to learn. We hit so many joints and bought so many cocktails for anyone and everyone that we're honorary members of the distillers council. We may not have receipts for our binge, but we spent close to a grand."

I had a few benders under my belt. Of course buying drinks for the entire drinking public was not my style. Still, a thousand bucks for a few nights in bars was a bit much. I said nothing.

John/Juan was pacing and loudly talking. "We got lucky, we know it."

"Lucky, we know it."

"Yes, we were throwing around money, drinking champagne, and talking about the congressional race. Our line was 'Something's weird here, we hear the fix is in.'

"In one dump a drunken old dithorderly drethed in a ghathly gown and long gloveth puthed up to the bar next to uth. The face was worn to put it nicely. But the thmile, that wath pure evil.

The poor thing moaned, 'I'll buy, boys; champagne is it?"

His twin said, "We pounced. The lady was escorted to a table. That is, we each took an arm and steered the drunken bag to a chair. Talk about a lurch - we almost lost our benefactor as she fell off to port. We got her straightened and held on.

A drooling speech followed. 'Watch your hands, fellas, this ain't free stuff. Come over to my table, we'll have our drinkees.'

After reminding the unshapely sponge that we were already at her table, we each had a flute of champagne. There was a bit of a lull as our new pal got her mess in order. Then, surprisingly, a somewhat sober, and lucid presentation came.

'My name is Aunt Verda; life is a mirror and I'm a reflection. I know a lot about nothing. Oh, shit, you asked about the Congressional, what are you cops, investigators, FBI, railroad dicks? What's the deal?'

"That question comes often," we told her. "Dear lady, we are none of the above. Do you know the Bureau of Virtue? We are special agents. Fair elections and hair pie is the game."

'That's flying bullshit. I sell information myself.' She was listing again.

We Lawns never hesitate, "Indeed, indeed…we buy it. Quality is most important."

Aunt Verda pulled a large manila envelope from the bodice of her frock. 'I have pictures for sale. Others have bought them so the quality is good.'

"Really, who bought your snapshots?"

'Not so fast, Whitey' she snapped. We tried to stare her down but she was well rehearsed. 'Here's the deal. For ten grand you get the pics - you can inspect one first. There are three. For an additional grand I'll answer your questions.'

"We took a peek and instantly recognized one of the immortalized Congressional candidates. In a chorus we said, 'It's a done deal.'"

The boys were now doing a bit of a modified ballet. "Thonny, here are the pictureth. You may or may not be appalled. We aren't, life is often bizzare but convention ith for conventhoneerth."

I took a look. I wasn't anything but fascinated. The Demo candidate was having sex with men - multiples it's called, I think. Not my thing, but others might like these shots a lot. I mean they were erotic, not to me, mind you...oh, shit, I dropped my thoughts. "And?"

"And it is not classic blackmail but a clever mutant. These pictures are going to elect your next congressman - a chump without a chance will slither with the other snakes in Washington."

I asked, "How will it work?" and got a shouted reply, "We don't know yet. Thonny, this is big time... and tho's your old man." They cackled in unison.

The Lawns left me flabbergasted. It was not a time for the phone to ring - so it did. After the evening's events nothing could shock me I figured as I put the phone to mouth and ear. "Hello."

"Sonny, I've been trying you at home…it's too unreal, they eloped."

"What? Who? Astrid?"

"Our parents, you ass."

* * * * *

It was to become a favorite in their inventory of friendly disagreements - who said it first? The question being who proposed marriage?

"It is not a part of your cool demeanor, dear…ladies wait to be asked." Codfish grinned at her.

"But, W.T., you dropped me at the door - we were laughing about your two preposterous reporters. I said, 'We laugh well together - let's keep doing it.' You said, 'Alright, we will,' and I said, 'You're on.'"

A playful Codfish offered, "That was not a proposal, not an agreement, just foreplay."

Anita came back, "I joked, 'Wait, I'll pack some things.'"

He laughed, "And so you did."

"To get married, as I told you."

"As I invited you."

Codfish was glowing, "We're going to Reno to be married - I'm not sure how it happened. I'm as happy as I can remember. Whatever you want, I'll get it for you."

Anita purred, "What I really want is to try you on. Should we marry without having sex first?"

"I can pull over, there's a rest stop just ahead."

They stopped once in Auburn for gas and some teen-like necking while the tank filled. Inside both heads were similar thoughts, differently expressed.

"I will see how it works...an adventure is overdue. If this one doesn't do it, it will be the last man for me. He is quite nice, and funny. I hope he can do me proper."

"She is what I need for the long haul. Fantastic looks and mind. She'll be fun and take care of me. It's time for Codfish to swim with the current. And I desperately need to see her naked."

The elopers didn't know nor would they have cared that their children shared the incredulous turn of events over a pizza. Astrid was unhappy. No, she was livid. Her mother was bewitched or worse. She seemed to blame Dad.

I let her rant while carefully examining as much of her as I could see. She didn't notice or care. Boy, was this girl something and boy, was she pissed off. I thought to myself, "I'm the one who is bewitched." I took a stab, "They know what's up. Jesus, Dad certainly has seen it all. I mean, he's experienced."

She stared holes in my face. I struggled on. "You know what I mean...he's a man of the world."

"Oh, Sonny, tell me what that means." She laughed a bit. "Are men of the world a superior strain?"

I vowed silently, "She will not upset me - I'm going to handle this." I grinned, lowered my voice and tried again. "Look, Astrid, women control men, they do it with sex, money - they have most of the big dough, and the smarts. Guys are along for the experience, the fun, whatever. I know you girls run the show, it doesn't bother me. Your mother, whom I really like, will run my dad and he needs it." Talk about bull and she knew it.

"Jesus, Sonny, that's a load of crap." She watched my face fall. "I mean, it's so much more complicated …when you grow up you may get it."

I turned my head to hide my pleasure - maybe she was taking an interest in this immature lad. "Astrid, crap or not, the fact is women rule if they want to and that happens in all relationships - have one and you'll find out."

"Maybe so, what's our relationship now?"

"What do you mean?"

"Are you my step brother? That's what I mean."

I pondered that and guessed, "No."

"Lawyers should know these things, will you look it up?"

"Certainly - hell, I doubt it."

"Well, if we are sort of brother and sister, that ends whatever got started."

I bit, "What's that?"

"I will not be a party to incest…you shouldn't even suggest it."

I laughed, "But I didn't."

"But you want to."

One final try. "Look, Astrid, you've jerked me around enough. Someday we're going to collide and that, like everything else, is your call."

"Right. As far as you're concerned, Sonny, it's always my call. Don't forget. As to our parents, we should be supportive I suppose."

I said, "Yes, how?"

"Start by getting the negative crap out of your thoughts. Celebrate them."

"I have no negatives, you do, I'll celebrate, don't worry."

She wanted to go home so I, the flumoxed young man, took her. I took her to the door, received and returned a full-bodied kiss and left wanting more. The girl had gone silent for the last ten minutes we were together. Regarding her thoughts, I hoped I was in there somewhere.

* * * * *

She had a throaty laugh and was it engaged. "Boy, is this corny," Anita laughed again.

Codfish laid on the fish eye and pulled into a parking place marked "Participants." The little white stucco house was advertised as the "Now or Never Wedding Chapel."

He said, "Some fucking chapel."

"Stop it," still with a laugh.

They got out of the car; he had made it half way around to do the gentlemanly thing but the laughing bride to be had jumped out of her door. She stood smiling and smashing; he was overwhelmed. The red hair was all red today. The few grey strands had been retired. She wore it at shoulder length because W.T.

liked that. The vibrant figure was encased in a finely tailored suit, sort of an off green and there was a matching mauve purse and shoes, what could a guy say?

Except, "You are a gorgeous bride-to-be."

"You're not so bad yourself." And he wasn't. Black cashmere jacket, brown slacks and his "gator shoes." A white shirt framed his tie which was shaped, colored and painted to resemble a cod.

Anita had met the awful tie when he first came courting. Her comment to herself was, "That thing is doomed." She said nothing on her wedding day but maintained the thought, "Where did he get that stupid thing? It's gone as soon as we get home."

Codfish opened the door to his new life, as he figured it, and they entered the sacred parlor which was dominated by a blaring TV. A pock-marked young man was watching a quiz show. He jumped up, "Welcome folks, the Reverend is out back if that's what you're here for."

Codfish smiled and quickly said, "We want to get married, now."

"You bet, sir, we have this here form for you. And here's the rate sheet, you can get various levels, see?"

"Various levels of marriage?" Anita weighed in in a friendly way.

"No, ma'am, not that. No, just levels of service. Music, flowers, gold edge certificate, it's there on the sheet. I'll get Dad—'er the Reverend."

The couple smiled, kissed and giggled as they checked the rate sheet. Codfish said, "When in doubt, go for the full package."

"I'm not in doubt, W.T., but can we afford it?"

The reverend came into the room with a woman right behind him. "Good afternoon, friends, may God bless you. I'm Reverend Marvel Locust, this is Mrs. Locust, uh, Bambi, and you met my son, Luge." The minister smiled…a holy smile.

Hands were shook and acknowledgements made. Codfish asked for "the best there is," and that was greeted with a super holy smile.

"Since you folks came alone we supply the witnesses. So, ma'am, Bambi is your witness, attendant, maid of honor, whatever you want to call her."

Bambi, as if on cue, blurted, "You can call me anything, but don't call me late for dinner." She laughed, followed up with an imbecile's grin, and clapped an unprepared Luge solidly on the back. The young man lurched into the Reverend who gave the kid a not so friendly cuff to the jaw.

"Jesus Christ," mumbled Codfish.

Anita was laughing again, but nothing stopped the Reverend Marvel Locust, this was his production.

"Now the groom will be attended by Luge. He's the best man, if you will." He liked that phrase, "if you will," he'd heard it on TV.

Codfish turned to the kid, "How old are you?"

"Twenty-seven."

"Kiss my ass," Codfish blurted. "Make that seventeen."

"No sir, I just look young."

"You look like a moron."

"Stop it, W.T." Anita was laughing again, loudly.

"Oh, for Christ's sake, let's get it over with. I'll never forget this." Codfish was not hard to read at the moment.

The Locusts gathered together and then spread to their appointed stations. The wedding took less than three minutes.

"You may kiss the bride."

"I don't need your permission, your Grace." Codfish gave his wife a chaste buzz. Anita hung on to him and forced something more meaningful.

Forms were completed, money changed hands and the laughing bride left with a small bouquet and a large husband. Anita felt reborn and W.T. felt loved and in love. It had been so long.

"That was romantic," she whispered.

"What was?"

"Having a wedding party made up of aliens." She laughed. "My first wedding was small, nice and an elopement, too, but the aliens were Swedes."

"Swedes and aliens are the same thing." He grinned at his bride.

"And yours?"

"The works. Dear Pooh was rich, though she rarely advertised it. For her wedding, however, she went all out. Our only disagreement was over the champagne.

She wanted vintage and I said, 'Surely not for this crowd.' She had the best."

"Where now, husband?" She was in the middle of the front seat with her head on his shoulder. "Do I get a honeymoon or do you have to go back to the factory right away?"

"You get what you want - that's me, right? We're going to the Mapes - a hotel casino where I've lost several things over the years. Have you been there?"

"I've never been to Reno - does where we go matter to the cod?"

"Me…oh, him. He says, 'I'm here to please.'" He gave her a smug look.

"Please him you mean."

It was the best suite available which meant it was the best suite. The newlyweds stayed in, ate in, and played in.

"Not bad for an old fart." W.T. was sitting on the side of the bed having finally wilted for good.

"Why call me an old fart?" she laughed.

"Not you, me, sweetheart. You have the energy of a fifteen year old…and you're seemingly amenable to all of my crooked paths."

Anita didn't hesitate. "I have a mental age of eight or nine. So I just do what I want to. I like sex, you remind me that I have been away from a man too long. I didn't punish anyone but myself. Thank you, darling, you've rescued me."

"Anita, you're my rescue. You're my St. Bernard, no little cask hanging down but other goodies sure are."

"Stay away from poetry, dear." She reached for him.

The fun couple was back in the city after a couple of days. Astrid and her mother put together a modest reception by my standards. In other words, light on alcohol. Mother and daughter loved it. Dad was glowing more than his bride. Boy, was there gossip about this couple!

Astrid seemed pleased with the party, at least she was smiling. That's until I came into range. She hadn't ignored me exactly, after all, we'd talked on the phone a couple of times. But I hadn't been with her, and it wasn't for trying, since our pizza date. I gave her my sincere look, "You look like you need a break."

She drilled me with a cold stare. "From you? From life?"

"Jesus, take it easy, Astrid. I'm just trying to help you out."

"You're just trying to get after me."

"That too." There was no reason to lie. Finally I was blessed with a half smile. Was she gorgeous!

I pressed on. "I can make you really laugh if you'll go out with me Sunday."

She said, "Details, please."

"There's a lawn party in Tiburon. Usual crowd of phonies, climbers - rich neer-do-wells. But the attraction, guaranteed entertainment, will be going with us." I smiled.

"Please get it over with, Sonny." She was inspecting the other guests.

I plunged on, "LIVE/DIE has two investigative reporters, identical twins, Juan and John Lawn - they are smart, funny, and outrageous. I have to entertain them so Sunday's the day. When you meet these guys you'll break up."

She thought a few seconds, "John and Juan, are you kidding?"

"No." My superb grin was served to the lovely lady.

"The Lawns at a lawn party. Sonny, honey, you do have a bit of flair."

That was the first time she called me "honey"…a moment to savor. Of course she called a lot of people "honey."

CHAPTER 9

Just to be mean, I had the top down as we drove through a thick fog which had settled on the Golden Gate Bridge. The Lawns were perched on the back seat seemingly enjoying or at least tolerating the cold and wind. Next to me was the impossible Astrid, looking and acting as composed as she was.

The Lawns had waited in front of the Fairmont for us to pick them up. Were they staying there? Who knows? Not on the LIVE/DIE expense account I hoped.

Astrid had her first belly laugh of the day when the boys approached my car. They wore red straw hats and what looked like referee's shirts, the ones with black and white stripes. Next came pale yellow pants which stopped at their calves. Pedal pushers, to be precise. Traveling downward there were no socks. On their feet were bright red rubber gardener's clogs. Each little man carried an oversized straw bag with a stenciled portrait of J. Edgar Hoover on one side.

They didn't wait for doors to open. My guests, with an impressive show of agility, vaulted into the back seat. I noticed the Fairmont doorman had both hands over his face, his body was shaking.

I sort of made introductions; it was awkward because I couldn't tell my guests apart. The Lawns helped out so names were straight at least at the beginning of our outing. Astrid, a physician trained to cope with and treat all types of bodies, personalities and whatevers, rolled her eyes at me and almost lost it.

It's impossible to have a conversation in a fast-moving open convertible, thank God. But on the Marin side of the bridge as we slowly crawled through the town of Tiburon, the Lawns leaned forward and started on Astrid.

"We agree that your mother is a most handsome woman."

"Yeth we do."

Astrid, surprised, turned in her seat. "Do you know my mother?"

A sly looked passed between them. John or Juan had the ball. "We have met her only once, but we will always remember her loveliness. On that occasion Mr. Codfish was with your mother. Now that they have married my brother and I are planning a big surprise for them."

"Big thurprise," shouted the other one.

My turn. "What kind of surprise?" I asked.

"You'll find out, Thonny."

An echo, "You'll find out."

They tittered, grabbed their J. Edgar bags and clutched them close as we pulled through the gate of one of the finer estates in our little corner of the world.

The *faux* adobe hacienda had every possible touch of old California life save horse droppings and a Spanish language code. This layout was owned by the social climbers, Gunny and Bunny Weesel. Gunny put it without elaboration, "Objects are life, my life is an object." Not exactly captivating, but it suited his limitations.

The Weesels owned, ran and maximized the most prominent European antique gallery in San Francisco. While in the worldwide antique business their share was a pimple, that didn't mean our host and hostess didn't do damn well. The huge house, separate guest quarters, pool and tennis court shouted success. A generous lawn ran from the patio behind the house to a cliff where, if you jumped, you'd land in San Francisco Bay. The lavish grass plot had to be fifty yards long and maybe half as wide. Today the green slope was adorned with round tables sporting pink striped umbrellas. Six or eight could be seated at each set-up.

We followed other arriving guests through the house and onto the pool patio. Two bars and an elaborate buffet were placed around the edge of the tiled surface. In the center of the mini plaza was plenty of open space and it was needed. There had to be a couple of hundred people hanging around, some of whom I even recognized.

"Why are we here?" Astrid asked innocently.

"Relax," I sort of begged. "I like nice things, you know. Their gallery has been one of my sources for a couple of years." I gave her a firm nod.

"Is that a lot of business for them?"

"Not really."

"But you're on the A list." She raised her eyebrows.

"I don't know, shit, sorry - maybe I'm being set up for the big hit."

"Smart boy you are. I'll bet you won't bite."

"Not without your approval."

He was on us before we knew it. Gunny was as quick as an escaped hamster. *"Buenas tardes,* Sonny, glad you could make it."

Our host was short, round and the owner of an ill-fitting hair piece. Viewed from above by those of average height, the fawn-colored creation was shaped like a male athlete's cup. It didn't seem to matter to the targets of Gunny's avocation as women liked Gunny and Gunny loved women. He just had to use his hands to show how he cared. I introduced him and he grabbed Astrid's hand and then worked both of his up her arm.

"Wow, I know we haven't met, I'd never forget you." He worked on a spittle decorated leer.

Astrid couldn't shake his hands which were doing a bicep-tricep two step. Her voice wasn't pleasant. "You have an interesting home, Mr.—er."

"Call me Gunny." Suddenly his hands dropped to his sides. Over Astrid's shoulder he'd noticed the approaching Bunny. She scared the shit out of her husband and not just because she physically resembled a dock worker. The woman pulled in and we had a foursome for a minute or so. Bunny towered over her husband and had a tongue as sharp as a serpent's tooth, to borrow Dad's time-worn phrase.

There was a polite exchange of nothings until our hostess graciously asked of me, "Did you bring those two weirdos with you?"

"Uh, yes, I mean are you talking about the Lawn brothers?"

"I didn't get the name," she sneered, "but those assholes already have the party in an uproar. Will you please get them out of here?"

"Jesus, Bunny, take it easy." Gunny was in play. Even though he'd taken several steps backward, away from his wife, he had reluctantly decided to test his failed manhood.

She snarled, "Shut up, you dwarf, this is my biggest summer party and I'm fucked if I'm going to turn it into an episode of 'Star Trek.'"

I said, while putting on what I hoped was a totally insincere expression, "We'll be on our way. But, Bunny, please tell me what the problem was or is."

She quickly reviewed the situation, you could see it all over her mule-like face. "No, no, please stay, Sonny. I'm so nervous today. It's nothing, really. Some of our staff, male staff, are just ga-ga. They're, ah, interested in your friends. I mean nobody's working. The shitheads are just staring and gossiping among themselves. I don't know what to do." She trailed off and appeared to be in a modest retreat.

I glanced at Astrid, she had an undisguised evil smile and what looked like true hatred in her eyes.

Gunny chirped, "Stay, Sonny, stay Astrid. Sonny, tell Bunny what these guys do."

He didn't have a clue about what the Lawns did; Gunny was just trying to keep the lid on. So I got my chance. "The Lawns are renowned investigative reporters. They are working for LIVE/DIE magazine at the moment. I wanted you to meet them, Bunny, they're working on an expose of fraud in the local antique trade."

"What!" screamed Bunny. Gunny grabbed her arm and started to wheel her away.

I answered his quizzical look with a, "Just kidding." I'm not sure he heard me.

We got drinks and did the lawn...Astrid was most unladylike in her comments about Bunny suggesting at one point that "that bitch should be tarred and feathered."

We spotted Juan and John at a cliff-side table. As we watched, they fussed around a bit and then placed their absurd bags on a couple of chairs. They headed back up the lawn toward the spread and the bars. Boy, did they turn heads.

Astrid and I took our mother's helpers to an empty table which was close to where the Lawns would be. At least so we thought. While the boys were in deep discussion with a bartender, their table came under attack or, rather, their bags did.

A party of six approached the Lawn table.

"This is where we sit," bellowed a huge man whom I recognized. He casually threw the Lawns' bags on the grass and directed the seating around the table.

The big guy had a loaded plate and something green in a glass. He was accompanied by his double, that being his identical twin. The two giants were Ferd and Tird Donkee, who were well-known for their tasteless television ads. The twins featured themselves dressed in pastel tuxedos announcing, "Cheap cars for cheap folks." Donkee Motors had the franchise for cars like

Panhard and Wartburg. Nobody else wanted to represent so-called "off" or "shitty" brands but risk-taking had its rewards. There were plenty of off-brand and shitty car buyers.

The Donkee brothers had gone to Humboldt State College where they majored in football. Size counts when playing on the line, but a modicum of skill helps. Ferd and Tird were hopelessly uncoordinated and far from bright, so they always played second or third string and knew no heroics on the field. That didn't stop the giants from making up stories about their football exploits which they lied about to this day.

Humboldt State gave the brothers a couple of things...diplomas in physical education and wives. Their first years in foggy, rainy, boring Arcata took a toll. The boys had little social life beyond beer drinking with other brain dead student athletes. Then came the miracle. The Donkees spotted them during registration week. Were those chicks tough! Tall girl identical twins, with undisguised good bodies, showed their stuff. The girls had pleasant peasant faces with large noses; the Donkees could live with the honkers. And they did.

Nikki and Vikki Hinee were straight off the farm - dairy that is. There is something about girls and women who are in that udder and milk culture. It surfaced in the Hinee girls. Simply put, they attracted mouths and hands. Ferd and Tird were fumbling and over-eager suitors but the girls led them to home plate and eventually a double wedding.

145

Without Nikki and Vikki, Donkee Motors would be as dead as necker knobs. The women were smart and capable and knew their husbands' place which was anywhere but in the office. No deal, sale or whatever could be done without a Nikki or Vikki approval, and the foursome prospered accordingly.

The Donkee brothers and their dairy delight wives sat down, each with a major part of the buffet on their plates. But their helpings were modest compared to those of the third couple. Two older citizens literally had mountains of food some of which fell off their inadequate plates. When a scrap or stray morsel hit the table it was quickly scooped up and eaten. Farmer Hinee and his wife were in food heaven. Using their well-developed fingers the old milkers shoveled it in without pause. They nodded at their daughters from time to time as if to say, "Thank you," in cow language.

Astrid, in a not so subdued voice, noted, "It looks like those two seniors just got out of a slave labor camp. Who are they?"

I replied, "Refugees, I guess, the giant slobs are car dealers and those amazons are their milk maids."

Yes, I should have known. There had been enough hints that the Lawns just didn't fuck around and it was obvious when they came down the slope at a trot. Each lad carried, using both hands, what looked like and was a fish bowl. The salt around the bowl rims glistened as did the massive drink in each vessel. The boys had arranged for gargantuan margaritas. They sort of hopped toward their J. Edgar Hoovers and sat down on the lawn near where the bags had been thrown by the Donkee.

John and Juan said nothing that we could hear or see. They just attacked their stupendous drinks. The slurping and burping was certainly audible and judging by the angry stares from the six eaters at the table plenty annoying. After a few minutes the crudeness was accompanied by loud and prolonged emissions of wind. It was a brutal combination I have to say. This display finally took its toll on either Ferd or Tird. The Donkee tried to push his chair back without lifting it. That was a mistake. The chair legs caught in the grass and stayed put. Momentum took the lummox backward, and as he tipped his feet flew up and caught the underside of the table. Over it went. All plates, food, glasses, drinks and miscellany flew onto the two old dairy folk. Without pause the seniors started picking stuff off their clothes and eating it.

The Lawns jumped up, ran a few steps and dove on the fallen Donkee. Each little guy grabbed a large ear; their twisting was merciless.

"You're a rouge and a vagabond. You took our table. You touched our bags," John or Juan was yelling. Their captive was yelling even louder.

The ladies sprang into action, kicking at and scoring, I might add, on the Lawns. The guys kept ear twisting and then one went for Donkee eyes.

"Do you want me to rip his eyes out, honey?" This was John or maybe Juan.

Nikki and Vikki backed off. They started screaming, "Police, call the police."

147

"Murderers, they're killing him."

"Let him go, you pricks!"

I wondered why the abused twin's brother didn't join in. Maybe he always just left everything to the brains of the outfit.

Later Astrid claimed she had yelled at me several times. She said she begged me. All I heard her say was, "Sonny, do something."

I went over to the brawl and quietly told the Lawns it was time to go. They released what surely would become cauliflower ears and went over to fetch their infamous bags. I approached the women who were both red-eyed, hyperventilating and obviously furious. There could be a problem so I turned on my lawyer act and gave it a go.

"This was just terrible, are you ladies okay?" They seemed to nod. "I'm Sonny Brac, my friend and I saw this whole ugly episode."

"So what, kid, these two midgets are dead meat." A loyal wife spoke.

This wasn't going to be easy. I pulled a card out of my wallet. My practiced grim expression took over; I tried to sound stern. "Here's my card. Read it if you can. I represent these gentlemen who were flatly provoked by your conduct...and I mean all of you except those two Kurd refugees (who, by the way, were still eating). If you think you want to do something about this have your lawyer call me. And, bye the bye, you've just mistreated two of America's most famous and renowned investigative reporters."

I turned and walked away halfway expecting some kind of assault. We made our exit without explanation as our host and hostess were engaged in what appeared to be a bitter, bitter fight.

All they did was giggle. The three of them, I mean. The ride back to the city was all laughs. Astrid smiled at me from time to time. Then, just as I was about to try a clever riposte, a smirking laugh would erupt from the back seat and I would lose her as she joined in.

At last I pulled into the circular drive in front of the Fairmont. Astrid jumped out so the Lawns could exit.

"Thanks, Sonny."

"Thanks, Thonny."

I was tongue-tied but the Lawns still had more. They launched into a song...

> "Rootie toot toot, Rootie toot toot,
> We are the boys from the Institute,
> What we don't do is we don't screw,
> And we don't go with girls that do."

The twins each got a kiss from Astrid, then the threesome had a final laugh together. She was back in the car, flushed and obviously feeling just fine. I waited. She mused. I didn't want to tinker with her mood, but, hell, there were things to say and the drive to her place only took ten minutes.

"So, a good day, huh?"

"Sort of."

"What do you mean?"

"You're really distant, Sonny. You barely touch me."

"What, Astrid, does that mean?"

"A joke, babe, a joke. As I've said, your time may come. I like John and Juan a lot. Let's see more of them. On the other hand your crowd is not mine. What a sewer."

"You're right about one thing." I tried for a measured voice. "It's agreed, my time with you will come...I'm going to do what it takes."

She seemed ready for that. "That gives me control. Right? I like that." She nodded her head and the red hair flew.

I double-parked on Union expecting her patented chaste kiss. Instead we launched into some interesting necking...Astrid started it as I recall.

"Come on, we're going inside." She didn't look at me as she opened her door.

"I'll park." I was charged or whatever you say when you can barely contain yourself.

She had to be anxious too. "Leave it here, turn your blinkers on. Let's go!"

We ended up on the living room rug, at her direction. I took a great deal of pride, or self-satisfaction, in my measured approach at these moments. Well, nothing was measured this time. Astrid and I were all over each other, until she rolled away.

"Hey, sweetie, come back." I had elevated my head and propped myself on an elbow.

"No more, Sonny." She talked to the fireplace.

"I'm over here, look at me…this is meant to be, and so are we." Corny, no doubt, but, Jesus, was I in distress.

"Sonny, guess who's attracted to you. I mean really attracted. But that's all you get tonight…a modest ego boost to go with the fun. I have to be sure about you. About us. Being in control isn't enough."

I got up, walked a few steps to her, looked down, sat down and manufactured a long, deep sigh. I touched her back and tried for a pleading voice. "Okay, okay, but don't drag it on too long. Remember Nixon…? He was in control but look what happened."

CHAPTER 10

The Lawns were in their self-described "gopher mode." That is, they just kept digging. Dirt really flew when they got near Aunt Verda. The original source of the damming pictures was a weird one even to the dynamic and seasoned ace investigative reporters. And no wonder.

Motreen Sulpha was a mere thirteen years of age when he started wearing his mother's panties. He clearly remembered the thrill of the first time he pulled a pair on. Also vivid was the disgrace when she caught him. Home from work early, the bitter divorcee just about pooped when she saw her darling Motreen clad in polyester panties and nothing else. The little fella appeared to be aroused but that quickly faded.

"What the hell are you doing? You sick pervert, you're worse than your father."

She went at him and the lad cowered into a fold on the floor of her bedroom. That was not a wise defensive move. The enraged woman proceeded to kick her son aiming up and down his skinny, white panty-clad body.

Motreen nursed his bruises and hate boiled. Some modest relief came from the thrill of the tightness of the panties he'd stolen from his bitch mother but this little partial family was not to be.

All the guy lived for was getting away, and that he did. A high school diploma, a fine collection of women's underwear purchased here and there, and a warning about v.d. from his detested Mom...that was the young man's legacy...he was on his own.

Motreen, hardly a boob, eased into civil service. To be exact, a clerk's position at the State Shoe Division. This bureaucracy had offices statewide because, as a negotiated perk, each California state employee was entitled to one free pair of shoes a year. Featuring the idiotic slogan, "We Just Try To Do A Good Job," the SSD was the ultimate government joke. But try to get rid of it. Shoes were sacred entitlements even though the inventory offered was such that nobody but shepherds and accountants would wear them. Originally these clunkers were made by convicts. After a suit by the ACLU alleging slavery and environmental hazards from leather fumes, the SSD caved and shut down its prison shoe plants. But it didn't shut down its program. This was a matter of self-preservation.

Following a trade mission led by the governor and peopled by the usual collection of charlatans, California gave its shoe manufacturing business to the Kingdom of Tonga. In exchange, the Golden State got exclusive U.S. import rights to Tonga's fermented coconut meat. To economize, the shoes and coco meat were shipped together in the same containers. After a long ocean voyage the foul coco smell permeated the shoes, at least temporarily. SSD stores smelled accordingly. It was a fact that state workers got hooked on the putrid odor. Some claimed it was an aphrodisiac or whatever.

So into the exciting state shoe world went the young, lovely Motreen. He was now tall, slender and oddly attractive to both sexes. This individual's raging hormones were as contrary as democracy and reality. He checked out various neighborhoods but Polk Street soon became his hangout. Gays had taken over the Polk Gulch area and that was the atmosphere the young clerk thought he wanted. That did not mean he wanted the sex…not for him, at least not yet. Despite constant entreaties, Motreen wasn't a player. Not when he could get it off by wearing panties and now, under his shirt, a bra.

Confusion, nice but still confusion, unexpectedly came at work. His desk had been next to an empty slot…for over a year now. And suddenly there was a girl. He first saw her on a Monday morning. She had a super smile, and from a distance appeared to be quite a looker.

As he walked to his desk she got up and offered her hand. Her smile was frozen, and she showed a real set of chompers. "Hi, I'm Verda Bush, I guess we'll be here next to each other."

"Uh, yeah…hello, I'm Motreen." He ungraciously plunked down on his state-issue chair.

"Well, is it Motrin?"

"Motreen."

"I see, anyway, maybe you can show me the ropes …this place seems so weird. I mean, what do we do?"

"Shoes. Shoes for state employees. They're entitled to 'em. One pair a year."

"Do they take them?"

"No."

Motreen was not being abrupt on purpose, the guy had been struck dumb since his first vision of Verda.

He rapidly organized his thoughts. "Succulent flesh! What a babe. I'd like to get ahold of one of her bras. Grand volcanos. And so's the rest. Minor flaw, yes, but beards can be dealt with."

The genetically challenged Motreen quickly launched a campaign to get the luscious creature. It only took a few dates, and a ton of pizza, and she was his. Could he afford to feed her? The beauty required at least one large pizza per day. That was starters. The beard and diet could be dealt with, Morteen was fairly confident of that. However, another flaw soon surfaced. Beyond question the girl was an imbecile. That was not all bad as she did as she was told. So it was a deal, she handed over her underwear and settled for occasional, dutiful sex. Lotions and salves appeared for an ongoing assault on the beard. It was a losing campaign.

A couple of years of living together, actually spending all of their time together, led to a solid bonding. Verda was in love and said it often. That embarrassed Motreen but he allowed it. The young man was in love too, but didn't or couldn't say so. The best he could do was pet her fondly, show her how her underwear looked on his skinny frame and encourage her to try to act as smart as possible, especially in public.

Filling a slot at the SSD was the perfect cover for an incompetent. The work, such as it was, was rote and undemanding. The only challenge associated with the farce was the effort to keep it going. SSD had to pretend to justify itself to the state legislature. Each year was a survival crisis. At the appropriate time, SSD director, Bo Nikee, would swoosh into Sacramento with his immense reserve fund in hand. Dinners, cocktails, whores - nothing was too good for the lawmakers.

SSD somehow survived and Mr. Nikee issued a lame "we've got to trim" ultimatum. Each State Shoe Store was told to cut personnel. Last hired, first fired - Verda had that dubious distinction in the San Francisco office. She also, by accolade, was honored as the office bonehead. But the pneumatic lovely was saved by Motreen. In his first exercise in the art of blackmail, the cross-dresser slyly mentioned to his boss that the man had been seen, more than once, cruising Polk Street. True, true. Boss man was in the closet; he needed to deal. Motreen offered a trade. Verda was to stay at SSD with a raise. The blackmailer would be silent. Bingo for Motreen; his avocation was born.

Verda told Motreen, after her job was saved, that he was "dry as a duck." Without asking for an explanation, the bra-wearing fella took it as a compliment. The girl was full of nonsensical little phrases, "headache of a mess," "impression on his face," "it's up what front that counts," etc. Motreen largely tuned out when the girl spoke as she wasn't wanted for her rambling nonsense but on occasion he did like her homilies.

Verda liked pictures, as she put it, and on most Saturdays she would walk down Van Ness Avenue to the Museum of Modern Art. Every week it was the same goodbye, "I'm going, Motreen, 'cause I like the pictures."

As if he was trying to stop her. He needed alone time with her underwear. "So long, sweetie, see ya later."

Not exactly, this time she was to become a headache of a mess. The girl walked slowly and aimlessly, looking around blankly. The bouncing babe was impervious to passing people, traffic, or reality. At a corner a tiny, old woman was poised to test crossing the street. She was using a walker.

"Hi, I'll steer ya."

"Say what?" screeched the senior.

"I'll help ya." Verda smiled and the dark shadow on her jaw became more prominent.

"No, no, get away, you mugger."

The light changed and the walker was launched into the crosswalk. Verda bounced along at the woman's side; giving protection was something the girl just had to do. The escort turned to face the old dear and found herself almost walking backwards.

A highly trained and motivated Sewer Department team had left an unmarked and uncovered manhole in the middle of the street. It became the scandal of the week. Verda went in backwards, did a half-flip and fell twenty feet landing on her head. The lovely old lady just kept going. She didn't want to get caught in traffic.

Verda's once luscious body was not discovered until two days later when the crew returned to work. Why the horrible omission?

Why this unnecessary death? The investigation was on.

Wouldn't you know it? The sewer crew had half a dozen civilian guests the prior Friday. The guys were distracted by their guests and forgot to put the lid on the hole. These guest visits happened from time to time in order to encourage citizen support for the Sewer Department. Most of the VIPs had given substantial sums to the Sewer Hospice Independent Trust. SHIT was the funding vehicle for golf tournaments, banquets and lunches, a dating service and other bennies for sewer workers.

The scandal of the missing manhole cover was front page and a relatively long-lived story. SHIT got an independent trustee, workers took things a bit more seriously and civilians were banned from helping things move along. The indirect cause of the tragedy, the lovable old lady with the walker, came forward to say, "I told her to butt out. Oh no, she just started walking backwards. She must have been feeble-minded."

Motreen was addled when Verda went missing. Two days and nights without a pizza; he was done, cooked. Then at the morgue the lovely body, topped by a badly mangled head, was his to see for the last time. He mumbled, "What bras she wore."

The young man was instantly a figure of sympathy and pity. A couple of his female co-workers offered solace and hinted at other things. He wasn't tempted. The depressed wretch tried to gather himself. He sorted and kept all of Verda's clothing that remotely fit him. Without any hesitation and as a memorial to his lost love, he decided to take her name - at least when he dressed as a girl.

His evolution was constant, steady and unhurried. Dresses were favored, but he also acquired skirts, sweaters, blouses, and shoes. An extensive Verda/Mortreen wardrobe was assembled out of love and need. Next to new shops were the haunt. Only the underwear had to be new and he chose racy and expensive goodies. How did a clerk at the State Shoe Division afford these luxuries? Not from his salary.

Motreen started small and got big - like most guys. He would pry a damning secret from a co-worker, then vaguely threaten to spill the beans. After a bit of a wait, Motreen would ask for a loan from the sucker. The money usually came. That was it. It never was repaid. He expanded operations having learned that petty blackmail easily worked among the barflies and losers that Motreen, now Verda, met in bars and clubs. Verda, a rather conservative cross-dresser, became a regular on the low-life club and bar circuit.

With time and the ravages of too many drinks, Verda aged into Aunt Verda, a vicious cretin. She sported faded silk frocks and an attitude. Long gloves hid stubby hands and hairy forearms. What she wanted, which was money, she got with her sharp eye and tongue.

Now here she was, toying with these unreal twin turkeys; and they had money.

When "the twin towers," as Aunt Verda slyly called them, dealt with weirdos, they became weird too…or more weird to be precise.

The fetid bar was the scene of yet another meeting. Aunt Verda drank and held court while as she mused to herself, "I'm holding the high ground."

The ace investigative reporters purposely cut their cocktail intake while lavishing refills on the long-glove wearing blackmailer.

It was gossip in the beginning...the twins wanted to see a drunken Auntie before exploring their business agenda. It didn't take all that long as the wasted old sot traveled life with a partial load on at all times.

"Did ya like the pics, boys? I got more."

"Really, thame catht?"

"No, not exactly. But I maybe could get 'em if you want."

"Yes, we're interethted...we want the thame guy, different catht...whatever. The price is the thame."

"Yes, yes, dearie...I'll check."

Juan or John continued, "A big bonus for our Aunt Verda can be earned, oh, tho eathily."

Verda perked up. "What's that?" With a drunken sweep, a gloved hand creamed her full glass sending it to the floor. Flying tequila and lemonade caught the virgin white jackets and shirts of the Lawns.

The fastidious little fellows were fit to murder. You just didn't "fuck with our clothing." And they so informed the chastened drunk. Back peddle! The high ground holder retreated downhill. Money could be had here. Close to sobbing, Aunt Verda laid on an apology again, and again. The Lawns dabbed away at their spotted duds and took over.

"Who bought the nasty pictures from you?"

These was no hesitation. "A man in high political circles," a pause, a sour look, "a Republican maybe."

"Name?"

"I don't know."

"Yes you do, dearie, and you'll tell becauth we'll pay. A modeth thum, that ith."

"How much?"

"Five hundred...we won't bargain, we'll walk firtht."

"Okay, it was Mr. Nicely. You're so rude." Aunt Verda sniffed.

"B.O. Nicely, the GOP chairman?"

"Yes, he called. Said he knew I had some evidence about Rommel - and then he bought it."

The other Lawn leaned across the table and grabbed a gloved wrist, Aunt Verda yelped, "You have such a grip, please." The squeeze intensified.

"It was the other way around, wasn't it? You called Nicely, right?"

"That may have been it, I'm confused."

"That is exactly what happened, case closed. Then you got the pictures from whomever. We want whomever, we'll pay, again five hundred. It's your chance to rekindle our friendship."

Aunt Verda was scared. The boys were very hostile. Who did they work for? They seemed like a couple of pansies but they could be muscle, dangerous muscle. So, decision time.

"The pictures came from a film studio. I won't have to be involved in this, will I?"

No answer.

161

Out it came. "It's Turf Sisters Productions."

"Uh, uh, tho the thudio gave you the lovely thmut?"

"Not exactly…a disgruntled employee was selling. I heard about it…I bought."

"And the negativeth?"

"Well, of course."

"We want them…today."

"Five thousand, if you please."

"We don't pleathe." Aunt Verda's wrist was seized again.

"Okay…all right…whatever's fair…that hurts."

"We'll give you a thou for the negatives…where are they?"

"With me - I'm quite careful, you know."

So once again the dissipated Aunt Verda stocked her cash account. The Lawns got what they came for …big time. It was a textbook commercial transaction, both parties were satisfied.

* * * * *

The only call I was interested in was one to or from Astrid. I had talked with her a few times after the Lawns destroyed the lawn party, but the girl was playing it cool or rather just not playing. I was rehearsing clever dialogue when and if I got a chance to use it when the phone interrupted my search for keenness. On the line was one of them.

"Thorry, Thonny, but thith ith thtarting to thmoke. We have the negativeth for the foul picth and better, their thource. This geth delicate."

"What do you mean?"

"The picth came from Turf Thithter Productionth. You know it, right?"

"Right - I mean, no."

"Heavy porno. Quality thuff, thown everywhere even the White Houth. Know the owner?"

"You got me."

"A rather famouth, lotta everything model is the head pornographer, owner that ith, Thonny."

"Okay - male or female?"

"The name ith Bergen Bode."

"Kiss my radish; are you sure?"

"Yeth, we're thure. She owns Turf Thisterth - whath behind that we're going to mole out."

"Yeh, you're on it. Holy shit. Do you need anything, any help?"

"We need money, we're buying our way on thith one."

"Okay, is five enough? I'll call Dede."

"Make it ten."

The Lawns were now beyond expensive. If Dad knew he wasn't complaining. I flashed on Dede Figueroa as I dialed the magazine. What a little vixen. And to think she could have had me.

She picked up and I tried to leer over the phone wire. "Hi Sonny, you are a stranger around here - at least to me."

"Sorry, dear, I'm working on a big case."

"Our date didn't work because of me - I think we should try again." She was purring into the phone.

Jack Tomlinson

"Dede, that's nice to hear, really nice. Listen, when this case is over I'm back...but now I need more expense money for the Lawns - ten grand."

There was a pause. "Are you being blackmailed? I'm serious."

"Come on, dear, cut a check and just be your glorious self."

"Promise you'll give me a second chance."

"I promise," I lied.

The Lawns' approach was the classic "rotten personnel" technique. Identify employees of the target. Find somebody who has a gripe no matter how petty. Turn the sucker against the target. Use money, false friendship, threats, whatever it takes. After a week, the Lawns had a Turf Sisters soundman in their pocket. A veteran of twenty feature length explicit art films, Lionel Fang met the Lawns, where else, at his local bar. The two ace investigative reporters were so polished Lionel caved early and cheaply. He spouted like a blow hole.

"These pictures are stills from the dubious hit 'Three Groins in a Fountain.' That young man is from Canada. He's here rarely. Our executive producer found him in Montreal - I think." Lionel had barely glanced at the photos.

"What's the name? Who's the executive producer?"

"'B.B.' is what she's called. She's the owner of the studio so they say. A beautiful woman, a model. I mean a real model."

Lionel earned his two hundred bucks and the free drinks. The Lawns hit the sidewalk and skipped up Bay Street holding hands. Before long they were singing, "Bangin' Away on B.B." They worked up new lyrics for an old favorite.

My first call the next day was from a Lawn. We had to meet so I was told. I felt a non-alcohol induced incident of morning sickness coming on.

"What's the deal, can't you just tell me?"

I heard a prolonged, loud and phony sigh. "Thonny, nothing, I mean nothing geth by Ma Bell. We'll do lunch."

The city was home to at least two restaurants where regular patrons could puff themselves by being recognized and, most importantly, buy recognition with a personal name plaque. These pathetic badges of bad taste were affixed on or near various tables and thus those needing recognition had their "own" tables. The less fortunate could dine at same, if available. It was a clever marketing ploy which appealed to the insecure, slaves of gossip columns and idiot savants.

CHURLISH not only had table plaques but it dripped with rudeness, bad service, ghastly food and a strange odor. The place was a smashing success especially among those wanting to be seen…by anybody. The Lawns were hep quickly and established themselves as honored patrons. The twins needed an upscale place to unwind from their investigation. After all, their efforts were, in large part, concentrated on meetings in scuzzy bars.

The ace investigative reporters were a fine match for the snobs who ran and staffed CHURLISH. The little men used time-tested methods to seize their beachhead. An imperious middle-aged man served as maitre 'd. Arrivals, except the table plaque set, were largely ignored, jammed into a small reception and subject to disdainful stares from the host and staff. Those who did not cow usually got a table after an unreasonable delay. This game was played with or without a reservation.

The Lawns faced the standard humiliation on their first visit. Boy, were they wizzed! They returned the very next day, clothed in fire inspector's uniforms.

John or Juan was first to the maitre 'd, "We want our table now. We'll close this fire trap otherwise. From this day forward, when we arrive, we're seated... until you hear differently." This was said through a multi-watt smile.

Nobody pushed the snotty host around. That was a house rule as well as putty to the man's facade. "I beg your pardon, little man. Your chief dines here and I'm about to call him. He'll take the call, he adores Fritzie, and you two will be painting hydrants. Step away now." He glared at the twins and then turned his back.

The thick reservation book soon missed a few pages. These were crumpled on the top of the maitre'd's station and set on fire by John or Juan. They shouted, "Fire...fire! Everybody out!"

Then, shouting in concert, came the old saw, "Women and children first!"

The maitre 'd looked aghast, because he was. He fluttered his hands in the direction of the bonfire but that was it. Diners in the front of the room could see and smell and a few quickly headed for the door. The majority of customers and staff were not in play.

A Lawn grabbed a couple of water glasses off a nearby table, doused the little fire and shouted, "Fire Department. It's under control. Enjoy your lunch... compliments of the house."

The maitre'd thought he was recovering somewhat except there was a pain shooting up his left leg. A fire inspector was standing on his foot and grinding a bit, too. The officer whispered, "Now be certain before you thpeak or act. Thith ith what happenth when you fuck with uth. Tho don't. Take uth to your bouthom and rewardth will thower you...be petulant and we won't be rethponthible. Now, aren't we your new favorite gueth, from thith day forward?" He jumped on the foot.

"Ouch, my God." There was a slight pause as the host looked for help which wasn't coming. "Please follow me, your table is waiting." And it was.

The ace investigative reporters soon loved CHURLISH, Fritzie and the impossible staff. When you can beat someone at his own game it leads to the best of times. Food was not important, drinks were, but the object was to be seen. And how could anyone miss these two? In a very short time the Lawns had their plaque and table and the admiration of the restaurant's staff and crew. After all, they spent like drunken sheiks, tipped better and always had a joke to share. The unlimited expense account from LIVE/DIE helped.

I went with them because a change of venue was in order and I couldn't shake their need for face to face meets. The meetings in my office were more vaudeville than business so maybe a quiet lunch would work. Wrong. I drove the Lawns to CHURLISH. My car, my escape, so I thought. The boys had suggested lunch, a chat and nothing else, but I smelled a big revelation. Besides, I wanted to see this restaurant where "everyone gets insulted and loves it," to quote an airhead newspaper columnist who was probably on the take.

I wore lawyer's blue with a too expensive shirt of a slightly lighter hue. Any originality was expressed in my canary yellow tie patterned with small replicas of the Great Seal of Andorra. I was wallpaper for the Lawns who had on Scoutmaster uniforms complete with sashes covered with dozens of merit badges. They wore service caps with "BSA" on one side and "Troop 7-11, Winnemucca" on the other. Of course, heads turned and of course, that was just what the boys were there for.

We were seated with big time ass kissing and hoopla. One of the twins gave the maitre'd several bills. I felt like I gave the tip, which was just about right. A waiter appeared, "Ya want drinks? Make it quick, I'm busy."

The boys tittered. "That okay, Ossie, the uthual for us. What about you, Thonny?"

I hesitated. Ossie, who looked like a giant panda, yelped, "What about you, Thonny? I ain't got all day."

More tittering.

I may or may not have looked cool. I tried to sound it. "Ossie, a bloody mary and for chrissake, zip up."

He looked down as his hand moved toward the front of his pants. I scored. I smiled, the Lawns howled and Ossie offered, "Ya got me."

"Thonny, remember we mentioned a surprith for the newlyweds?"

I nodded warily. They pointed to a silver plaque on the wall above our table. I leaned toward it and read:

> Mr. and Mrs. Codfish Brac
> Wealth, Obligation, Warmth

The other one took over, "So, Sonny, is it not class? Maybe too subtle but still effective. Get it? Take the first letters of the family motto, they spell "WOW.""

He smiled at me, they smiled at each other, then the entire dining room. I got it allright, in the form of a sharp wrench to my gut. The little men had crossed from their wild side to the serious and that was a capital botch. My immediate goal was escape but I suffered through a couple more drinks, a drooling Ossie, and a French dip listed on the menu as "Elk Spleen on a Hard One." I assured my hosts that the newlyweds would be surprised and honored by their gesture. "Perhaps the lovebirds would best like it if they came here alone…I mean the surprise and all." I was mumbling and couldn't help it.

"Good, Sonny, we'll hide at another table to watch their joy. Will you get a date? We'll take care of the rest."

I nodded and smiled. Ossie appeared and saved me from a verbal commitment. "There's baked Mexico, lead pudding, scalp me and cubanos."

John/Juan immediately ordered, "Three big ones and a bottle of cognac." Ossie grunted and left us.

I had to ask, "What are those deserts?"

A smirk, an exchange of knowing smiles and a confession. "How the fuck do we know? We take stoogies and frog juice, that's perfect."

Handling a huge cigar is not in my job description. Neither is more than one cognac. But I'm weak-willed so vice controlled much of my afternoon.

Nothing further was said about the surprise plaque - thank God. The Lawns were into their investigation, reviewing and chewing. A few of their besotted thoughts made sense to me which meant they probably didn't in the sober world. I strongly suggested we leave after the Lawns soaked their napkins with cognac and set them on fire.

It was late afternoon when the CHURLISH doorman bid us farewell. "Don't come back, pissants." That was a suggestion I could relate to. The Lawns never mentioned the disaster to me again.

CHAPTER 11

B.O. Nicely was put upon. He didn't like being summoned, especially summoned to meet at a bar which was hardly his place of choice. Worse, he was commanded to be at the meet by Topper Bello.

The Democratic chairman had howled on the telephone. "We have to meet - now. I'll be at Reno's, at four. You'd better be there."

B.O. drained his ginger ale and waited for what he wondered. It wasn't long. Topper slid into the booth - no drink order, no greeting, he just offered a fountain of words. "We gotta pull the plug on this shit - now. Roy's working for that magazine - LIVE/DIE, they're on to it. I smell it. We're fucked." The Demo chairman had an extravagant amount of sweat on his face. Today he had dressed down, no costume save a cowboy shirt with a large image of a scantily clad Dale Evans on the back.

"Hold on, Topper, hold on. What is your source for this drivel? I assume you have one." The livid B.O. mounted his best sneer.

"Yes, smart ass. Your source is my source. She called me, said the Republicans were out to screw the Demos. So I played along, or rather paid along, and got the whole story, or enough of it. The drivel, as you inanely put it, came from Aunt Verda."

B.O. managed a major look of disdain. "My, my. And so what? The pictures are real, no denying that, so it's just a matter of who releases them and when.

Granted, if Roy and his magazine gang get the story they may move on it. But that's hardly fatal to our cause. Nobody, and I mean nobody, in the media will print or show the pictures. Rumor will run the show. It might hurt if there are early hints in the press about your slimeball but it won't stop our righteous mission. You'll do your part and screw up any effort to get a successor to grimy Gunther. You've been rewarded, Topper, no Indian givers."

"Yeah, yeah. So if nobody will print the pictures, how does it get out?"

"Why, Topper, you and I hold a press conference at the appropriate time and we just hold the pictures up and let the boys and girls of the press have a good look."

"Fuck that, I want out, B.O., I shoulda never got in. Greed did me in."

B.O. leaned across the table. He whispered, "You're in, in so deep you're a flounder. Time to tighten your jock strap and finish the game. Have you started dumping on Gunther? Talked to anybody? Called anybody? Spent any of your newfound wealth? You know, Topper, you could be newsworthy yourself."

"Don't threaten me…your behavior is beyond a misdemeanor."

B.O. slammed his empty glass down. It stood up to the pounding and he momentarily toyed with doing it again. Topper had noticeably jumped.

"You once had guts, Topper. I guess you drank them away. You're in, you're sticking and you're playing your role. That's an order."

Topper closed his eyes, nodded and then held his head with his hands. B.O. slid out of the booth and left without a goodbye. He was sure he had the shithead locked in and more sure who the next congressman from San Francisco was going to be.

* * * * *

I took the call without having it screened which is my usual practice. A Lawn was panting on the other end. I was told that another meeting was in order and in half an hour they were in my office. This time they didn't walk in, their movements were more of a slow modern dance. I couldn't miss their gold patent leather shoes and, for Christssakes, spats. They wore matching powder blue suits with the usual white shirts, which framed gold ties with large blue letters, "U.C.L.A."

After a song and dance, I'm not kidding, the message was delivered. "Sonny," said Juan/John, "we have to move on the beauteous B.B. But we're taboo."

The echo came, "Beauteouth, taboo."

"Why?" I thought a single word appropriate.

"Well we could, but as those sports ruffians say, 'We don't match up well.' Our plenipotentiary should be the Honorable Sir Codfish."

"Dad? He's a newly wed."

"He doesn't have to bonk her." That brought us a moment of togetherness as we joined in laughter. It took a few more minutes for their recital, my agreement of sorts, and the exit number. They gave me a few stanzas of "The Last Time I Saw Split" and left.

For unknown reasons I skipped Mooneys that night and headed home. While I had little objection to the current current, I was a needy puppy emotionally. After a couple of drinks I looked for frozen or canned food. Whatever one thinks, it's still easier. The call and the declaration made me forget food and booze. "I'm coming over." It was that simple.

Astrid wore jeans, a sweat shirt, tennies, and her scrub room face. She walked by me after I opened the door and headed right for the well-stocked bar which happened to be the major item of decor in my living room.

"Do you have any cold white wine?"

"Sure, I'll get it...aren't you on your way to work soon?" I tried to look casual and sound casual while my mind raced.

Astrid seemed preoccupied. "It's my day off...I spent the afternoon thinking about you. Not so happily, I might add. The unanimous verdict is that you're a lying bastard who just wants to get in my pants."

"Whoa - wait a minute - let's start over. You step out in the hall and I'll open the door for you once again."

"Mom came by this morning to get some things. They're still living on that dumb ferry boat. Anyway, your name came up and she said and I quote, 'Apparently bedding Sonny Brac is quite the sport. He is extremely wealthy, way beyond what W.T. or anybody else has. Sonny has the best of all worlds - if you have few values.'"

I weighed in with, "Slander! I like your mother, now my stepmother. I like her a lot. But she doesn't know me, my values or how much I care for you."

"So what is your approach to women, Sonny? You find a girl or she finds you, you have her and you dump her. Why? I suspect you bullshit yourself that they're fortune hunters - all of them. It's convenient but so lame. Get a dog, it'll teach you about commitment."

That stung especially because it was mostly untrue in my objective view. I offered, "Somebody has a long knife out for me. Some evil force is trying to break up our inevitable romance before I get my hands on you."

I could of sworn she was going to stomp her feet - instead she hit the couch, bounced and stared at the ceiling. "I'm not interested in wealth, or your stupid, non-caring lifestyle. What have you got, Sonny? Vicious non-friends, disloyalty and failed love."

"Come on, Astrid, you're burying me." I was hurt but still a willing penitent.

"I like you, Sonny, I'm so disappointed that we come from different worlds, different lifestyles. We have different values."

It was my turn. "Horse doo doo, have you been watching pop shrinks on the boob tube? Look around you, you live nicer, better and more hygienic than I do, but our lifestyles aren't that different. You work, I work, we can spend our income, can't we? My moral code is no better or worse than yours - maybe not quite as high as yours, your righteousness."

I was getting warmed up. She had finished her wine. I went for a back-up.

"Stop the drinking."

"Altogether?"

"Drink in moderation."

"Okay, consider me reformed and I mean it. Now you owe me."

"What?"

"I very much want to kiss you."

"What do you really want?"

"To sleep with you."

"You want sex do you?" She smiled her way off the couch and pulled off her sweatshirt.

And I said, "Wow."

* * * * *

Codfish still had what he thought was her home telephone number. He rang. Disconnected. Then he called Turf Sisters Productions asking, as advised by the Lawns, for "B.B." This inquiry was met with a denial that such a person was there or even known. The ever resourceful Codfish changed tactics.

"My name is W.T. Brac, I'm an agent of the Internal Revenue Service, that's IRS, honey. You'll recognize B.B., she's the very tall, good-looking woman who runs your studio. When you see her tell her to call Mr. Brac. The number's three four four zero two five two. Got that? Good. This is very important. If she can't settle her tax problem, we're prepared to seize the studio today, and put all of you fine citizens out of work." He had left the number to his private line.

Codfish called his wife on another line and spent fifteen minutes talking about nothing much except bliss …they were interrupted.

"Hello, Bergen…pay your taxes."

"You're a smart ass, Mr. IRS."

"I needed to reach you, sorry, your receptionist is either well-trained or rather dumb…at least I got to you."

"What's the problem, Codfish? I thought you were happily married…that's the line in the gossip columns."

"True enough…I'm chasing you for another reason, not your great bod. I need to see you, reason to be explained, will you join me for lunch tomorrow?"

He heard her sigh. "What's the reason? I want dinner, tonight."

Codfish was careful now, he didn't want to loose her. "Dinner it is…and the reason is potential trouble that you don't want."

"What the hell is it? Tell me."

"Scandal, crime, your studio is involved. I'll tell you in person. How about the Palace Court at 7:30?"

Bergen snapped, "You're so set in your ways…old fashioned and too old to change. I hate that place and you know it." She hung up.

She also showed up. Watching the creature stride across the room was a temporary distraction for most of the diners. What a screaming beauty; taller than many males in the room she loped like a cheetah and her body moved accordingly.

Her pre-planned kiss on the mouth took Codfish by surprise but, then again, what fun. "You're one of the great broads as I've said to you more than once."

"Old people repeat themselves. You look good considering. What's she doing to you or rather how's she doing you?"

He grinned, waved for a waitress and the champagne arrived with her. "Skoal," a nod, then a stare from her former lover.

"That toast is new one," she offered.

"My wife is Swedish, I'm learning new customs."

"I'll bet...in my business you see a lot of acts from Scandinavia. Those kids have it down." She laughed and drained her flute in two large swallows.

"So, Bergen, is it your business? Do you run or own the city's premier porno film company?"

"I wouldn't limit it to San Francisco, we're number one in the country so I'm told. Anyway, I had to do something with my money - I scored after I left you."

"Scored?"

"I married - rich old devil wants model to molest. You should know the story, Mr. Brac. Anyway, I got a generous bribe to marry and a spectacular legacy when he died six months later." She looked away, was that a tear?

"I'm sorry, Bergen, this is all news to me. How did your husband die?"

"I'd rather not." She managed a wan smile, and they addressed the menu.

A second bottle of bubbly helped them ease into the meal and the woman started to talk freely. "I invested in the studio because it makes so much money it's obscene - just like our product. I'm not bothered with any of what we do. Our actors are protected - especially the girls. We have doctors, a psychologist, even a voyeur minister on staff. The kids do what they want, it gets filmed and we sell it. It's the American way."

Codfish gave her the fish eye. "Bullshit, but I'm not a fan. Frankly, I don't care - I'm not some Bible-eating politician. However, there is a matter of some concern. My magazine is profiling candidates in the special congressional race. Know about it?"

"Sort of."

"One of the candidates is in your work product, it seems." He cleared his throat. "I have pictures."

"Pictures we've got too, Codfish, thousands. Are yours dirty? Mine are." Bergen was smug.

"Will you take a look?"

"Jesus, why not."

Codfish pushed a manila envelope across the table. "I wouldn't pull those out here - we might be misunderstood."

She nodded, peered into the envelope, laughed, and excused herself. "A quick trip to the loo, dear."

And it was quick. Seated again, she drilled him. "What's the big deal?"

"The dark-haired one, on his knees most of the time. He's the Democratic candidate for Congress." Codfish was deadly serious.

It was a giggle what went into a huge loud laugh. The beautiful woman hid her face in her napkin. "Shit, oh dear. Codfish, that athlete is a Canadian switch hitter that we use from time to time. Actually my discovery...name's Ronnie, stage name Duke Hard." She wiped her eyes and shook her head.

"Where is Mr. Hard these days, do you know?" Codfish was not sounding friendly.

"Montreal maybe, I don't know. Is Ronnie your political candidate? Something is really screwy."

"Agreed. Can you find Mr. Hard for me?"

"Maybe, but why should I? This fun evening is anything but. You're a sour old fucker these days... excuse me, I'm leaving."

He quickly said, "Sorry, sorry Bergen. This is damn important...blackmail, election fraud, the works. The ammunition came from your studio. I didn't take those pictures, your people did. We're going to expose the whole filthy mess very soon. Turf Sisters Productions can be treated any number of ways...I can make sure it's at the lowest possible level of exposure. You won't be mentioned...the pictures have to be. Let's just call them publicity shots for a porno flick or whatever." He looked at her and raised his eyebrows.

"And all you want from me is Ronnie...is that it?"

"Yes, we want to interview him."

Bergen pushed her chair back and got up and uncoiled to tower over Codfish. She almost looked pleased, maybe it was the light.

"Who said journalism was noble? Your crowd has a homesickness for the sewer. You always end up there floating along with the other turds. So I'm blackmailed too, how magnanimous of you, Codfish. I'll get you some phone numbers," She headed out of the room, again followed by the eyes of most of the crowd.

Codfish had been hit…and it smarted. It was easy for him to continue drinking. He mused, "By myself in this grand room, it's not right." The instinct had not locked in, that is, among other things, wives give comfort, the ultimate comfort. He went home to the ferry in a cab, too drunk to drive. Anita laughed, took care of him and asked no questions. He was sober enough to realize the treasure he had.

* * * * *

I viewed our editorial meetings as Dad's play time. But even the feared Codfish needed to straighten himself out a bit when things got twisted. Before that day's big show, Codfish had ten minutes or so alone with Wally Moundminder, subject: Bergen Bode's mole.

Later Dad told me the man's defense. It was pathetic. Wally confessed that his perversion started years ago when he visited the arcade at Pier 39. There was a game where faux moles popped up in different holes and the player tried to whack them with a paddle before the mole popped back down. Wally was mesmerized. He became a mole junkie. From animal mole whacking to human mole whacking was not a giant leap for the Food & Beverage editor. Now he assaulted moles on humans. He couldn't help himself.

Dad concluded that the man had slipped his hawser, a ferry boat term I think. Anyway, Wally was a good liar and storyteller and magazines need that kind of talent. So Dad forgave him after a fashion. Instead of his white cane, Wally was sentenced to carry a battery-powered flashing yellow light at all times. Dad would review his conduct in sixty days.

At editorial meetings there were no assigned seats. So today I sat between Barbara Boring, who appeared to have waxed her moustache, and Dede, who appeared luscious. Dad had the table's end and across from me sat Roy and the Lawns. The little guys wore white jump suits, formidable boots and dark glasses. Wally stood in the corner with his flashing light strapped to his arm.

Dad was all business so it seemed as he frowned and growled a bit. Whoops, not as grim as I suspected. He fished for his briefcase and produced a gold coptic cross. Each of us got a wave in what I took as a blessing.

He said, "What have we got?"

"Dad, what have you got? Otherwise we're stalled." I didn't need another quiz show.

Codfish gave me the fish eye and took off. "We have the nefarious scheme. We have the dirty or rather shocking photos. What's wrong here, if anything?"

Barbara pounced, "Many people in this community are not as prudish as some in this room. The story is moron grade titillation. I'd run all the pictures with the header, 'Congressional Candidate a Good Host.' Make it a centerfold."

"All right!" Dad roared. "The issue is what to do with what we have. I mean the issue is what do we have? I had dinner with a representative of Turf Sisters." He told us the story and what was to be done about it.

The Lawns were dispatched to Montreal to find and interrogate the adventuresome Duke Hard.

I argued for the direct approach, "Let's show the pictures to Gunther S.S…what's to lose?"

"Maybe the story," said Roy. "Look, there won't be a stolen election, and that is the story. If Gunther drops out now the Demos will get a new candidate. The gate isn't slammed according to the election code. Candidates can be substituted until twenty-one days before the vote. So there are a couple of weeks yet for an alternate to step in."

"A judge might stop the thing," Dede hesitated.

I played lawyer. "Not likely. On what grounds? Face it, we don't have the complete story until Gunther talks. We have to ask him, don't we? If he drops out he drops out. We're first in line to publish a story whatever it is."

Roy eased toward a middle course. "I say move up publication, a special edition. We'll go with what we have, which is plenty. We cover with an editorial by Codfish which hints at the rest. Here's the truth so far, folks."

Dad said, "Any objections?" He didn't wait a second. "Okay, Roy, get it started. Alert the printer. Boys, find the missing mountie. Sonny, let's get to Gunther, in person. We close on this quickly or we'll be that object in that well-known punch bowl."

It was close to 10:00 p.m. when we were dismissed with a grand wave of the coptic cross. I left the meeting headed for the nearest phone to call Astrid. "It's time to take up where we left off," I hoped.

"I'm working graveyard as you know, or is there a memory problem?" She laughed. "Yes, Sonny, it was good, yes, Sonny, you are great, yes, Sonny, you can have more…but not two hours before I pull this shift."

"Okay, sweetheart…I need to talk with you…in person. Life isn't just sex…"

"Really? You're an unusual young man. Can you come over now? I'm alone. Can you come and get it?"

Codfish left the LIVE/DIE office and drove to the ferry. Anita had fallen for their accommodation. It was their first home and that meant a lot to her. She felt secure at night, even on the deserted waterfront. It helped that Codfish had an armed guard posted at the pier head.

Anita had held dinner, not that he asked. But it was appreciated on this night. W.T. needed care, more to his spirit than to his stomach, but the food helped.

Anita had it down from the beginning of their romance. Let this man think he's in charge. I'll respond and win only if I have to. She didn't have to scratch hard, the gruff exterior sheathed a sweetheart and she told him so - often. Tonight he made no false starts or excuses. Codfish sat down, slumped and let fly. If there was a theme to the tale it was disgust.

"I thought you liked this expose business, darling."

"So did I until I realized who was involved and what was involved." Codfish told her about Bergen, all about Bergen. He'd skipped that part when he came home smashed after he'd had dinner with the girl.

"You don't still carry that torch, do you? What is it?" She was standing behind the seated W.T. rubbing his temples.

"You're my torch...it's the porno thing I guess. I mean what if Astrid or Sonny was in that business? All those young people. Jesus, it makes me wanna puke." He got up and headed for the bar.

Anita spoke sharply, "You're upset because your Bergen fantasy turns out to be a human being. Americans are such prudes and hypocrites. The body is to be used and abused as the owner sees fit. You handle yours and let others handle theirs." She wasn't smiling.

"Okay, okay. Let's not have our first fight. I'm not a fucking prude, it's just a twinge of my old-fashioned morality, I guess."

"Crap, W.T...I'm going to bed." And she did.

Codfish fixed himself a mother's helper and proceeded to make up his mind. He called Roy, waking the editor up.

"Sorry, Roy, it's late, but I'm awake and now so are you."

"Yes, Codfish." The words came from an obviously half-awake speaker.

"I'll admit that I had second thoughts. This was out of hand, too ugly, something for the scandal sheets, perhaps. Anyway, screw it, we're going ahead - I'm determined."

A brave Roy asked, "Why did you call me?"

"Because you're the fucking editor. If anything goes wrong, you're the fall guy, got it?"

"Yes, sir." Roy hung up and went back to bed. His wife was awake.

"What is it?"

He sighed, "Must be a full moon."

CHAPTER 12

Roy thought he looked the part in his corduroy jacket, turtleneck, flannel slacks and desert boots. The editor was making a call.

He'd been up these steps so many times. The suite had not changed nor had the habits of the only other person in evidence. Topper Bello was in his office which was its usual mess. A tumbler of scotch had found a space on the cluttered desk.

"Howdy, Topper, you haven't changed your lifestyle since we last met." He nodded at the glass of whiskey.

"You'd be surprised at the changes, Roy."

"I've got news, Topper." Roy was smiling.

Topper took a pull on his drink. He was long past the point where a swallow of warm scotch made him grimace. He licked his lips. "What do you want?"

"First, to thank you for getting me out of here. You saved my ass." That got a nod, no eye contact.

"Anyway, maybe I can return the favor."

"Huh?"

"As you may know, we have the ace investigative reporters, John and Juan Lawn, working on a story for LIFE/DIE we're looking at the Congressional special to be exact."

"So?"

"Come on, Topper. There's a scheme to blackmail Gunther. The GOP may take the election and the seat by default. Gunther S.S. is going down. Heard about it?"

"No." The old man drained his glass.

Roy spoke softly. "I want to talk to Gunther, he's probably shitting his pants. His campaign stonewalls the press. You can get me to him, right? Are you on top of this? Are you okay?"

Roy had chosen the Topper route because he owed his former mentor and Topper could do Democrats like nobody else.

"Bothering Gunther is not a brilliant move, Roy. I mean, if there is scandal, corruption, it should come out. The public needs to know. But this one's bullshit. Your crazy story and your Mexican reporters are a bit much. Gunther is way ahead, read the papers, I'm not going to upset him with some yellow journalist crap."

"You'll want to rethink that, Topper, if you're a part of the scam, you'll fry, too."

"Get the fuck out of here."

Roy walked a half block to a pay phone. The call was picked up after several rings. "Rommel for Congress, Class not Gas."

"Hi, great slogan. Roy Incisor of LIVE/DIE Magazine."

"I'll give you press, hang on." He heard a muffled yell.

"Bobo Trout, press secretary, Roy. We met at some bar or another."

"Right, howdy, Bobo, I need to talk with Gunther asap. I'll bore you a second. There is a huge story about your man…we're sitting on it, but only for a last minute fact check. We're at the printers."

"So, tell me."

"In case you folks missed what's going on, your candidate is about to be ruined…smeared. We probably can stop the damage but Gunther has to participate."

"Roy, are you leveling here? This is hard to believe, to say the least."

"Set up a meeting, Bobo - we need Gunther today. We'll show him what we've got." There was a pregnant pause.

Bobo whispered, "It's off the record - got that? Ten tonight, our headquarters."

Roy hung up and called Topper - the old boy deserved another chance. No answer.

And no wonder. Topper Bellow was on his way. Full of scotch and angst he went off the Golden Gate Bridge late that afternoon. He was over the rail and into the air without hesitation. Feet first, the soon to be former Democratic Chairman firmly held his nose as he plunged.

* * * * *

Gunther S.S. looked and acted tired. Campaigning takes the starch out of a body. He perked up, to put it mildly, when I pulled the pictures out of the sacred manila envelope. I accompanied Roy to that meet for many reasons, the most important being because I wanted to. There had been some fencing. Bobo was adamant, "Off the record and no lawyers."

Roy was on it. "Off the record, you'll want lots of lawyers after you see what we've got."

The candidate was wearing a prison model orange jump suit, tennis shoes and oddly, a fedora. Was he ready to run, go for a stroll or shoot craps? He sat down and stared at the floor. After a long look, Gunther nodded indicating proceed. And we did. The pictures were in his hands. The poor bastard just about collapsed when he saw the goods. "No, no...Jesus Christ, no." He gathered himself a minute, looked around a bit wildly and blurted, "That my brother. We're identical twins. We have nothing to do with each other. I am so fucking mad I could set my hair on fire."

The candidate paused, apparently gathering himself. "So what's the deal here? Somebody want a payoff?"

"After a fashion," I replied, "it's said that these are pictures of you. They're going to be released right before the election. You'll be disgraced, you'll lose. The GOP takes a seat they've never held and never would but for these." I took the pictures and put them away.

There was the longest silence. Finally Gunther managed, "I'm broken, my shithead brother is broken... somebody's going to die."

Roy recited his well-prepared piece. "We have a lot, enough to send people, some big names straight to the DA. You're not broken necessarily. It really depends on how the story is played. If we do it straight

- that's an odd choice of words - the pictures may never get out."

Gunther was green or yellow on green and yellow. "I'm fucked."

Roy, most unkindly I thought, said, "That's your brother's line."

The meet gave us some confirmation of what we needed. But Gunther S.S. wasn't playing - yet.

After a night of no sleep and constant turmoil - and no Astrid - I got up early to call Montreal. The Lawns had called in with several contact numbers so I ran the list. Following a couple of no answers there was a pick-up and a deep male voice announced, "Mabel's whorehouse, Mabel speaking."

And why not? I was dealing with the Lawns.

A bit of banter produced one of our ace reporters on the line. "Thonny, the mithing actor ith thtill mithing."

"Keep at it and I don't mean at Mabel's." There was a mumbled acquiescence.

My report of the confrontation with Gunther brought a yelp and the words, "We'll be in the Thity of Saint Francith before the barth clothe." And they were.

John and Juan arrived at SFO at nine thirty that night. "We shit canned the search. Montreal is putrid." It was a given that the Lawns were peevish. By eleven o'clock they were drinking with Lionel Fang from Turf Sisters and pumping away. They called me and suggested a summit over breakfast the next morning. It was to be one of those meetings you never forget. The twins had turned Mr. Fang inside out. For three hundred and forty bucks plus drinks, they had hit a grand slam.

Duke Hard was in San Francisco, filming. Lionel saw the cat (his word) daily.

I traded my useless tidbit, "No, Dad hasn't heard from Bergen. He allowed, 'She's paying me back, the tramp.'" We agreed that it was obvious that we had to confront the star of screen and ream. We might keep his brother out of it…Gunther sort of deserved a pass.

After a breakfast where I had coffee and danish and the Lawns had tomato juice, tomato omelettes, grilled tomatoes and iced Ovaltines, we adjourned and agreed to reconvene in an hour at LIVE/DIE's office. There the group expanded to Dad and Roy. I insisted on being on the confrontation team. So did Roy, and so, half-heartedly, did Dad.

The Lawns just had a five star fit. First, Juan or John, climbed on the conference room table and started jumping around in a bizarre dance. He was wearing a pair of Canadian lumberjack boots - the ones with the little spikes. Birch chips flew. The other ace investigative reporter just yelled, over and over, "It'th our fucking thory."

Dad pushed his chair back, stood up and made a cross with his two forefingers. "The Lawns are our first team, we're sending them in alone and God help our righteous cause."

The two little brats stopped misbehaving, arranged themselves side by side and saluted Dad. They did a military about face and left the room singing, "Coming In on a Wing and a Prayer."

Puke on Duke, as the confrontation came to be known, went down at the Turf Sisters studio. The Lawns were tipped on timing by Lionel and arrived as shooting wrapped for the day. The boys waited in the reception, having asked to see B.B. Their calculated maneuver worked. Heels cooled while somebody figured what to do with the two tiny men who called themselves reporters and were dressed as lumberjacks. After a short wait, out came the target, who was flattered by the autograph request until he saw the picture being flashed by John/Juan.

"Hey, where'd ya get that?" The movie star made a grab for the photo.

The Lawns were not only quick but surprisingly strong - ask Aunt Verda. They grabbed Duke. "This isn't going to take long, Cowboy." He soon was seated on a couch with a Lawn close on either side. "We'll ask questions. Nod if the answer is yes, shake your head if it's no."

In five minutes they had Mr. Hard's confirmation. The Rommel brothers had gone their separate ways many years ago. Duke had posed for the damning pictures and many, many others. Not only did he make movies he also did just about anything else if it had to do with sex. He had no knowledge of the congressional race.

A Lawn offered, "Thanks, fella, do you have any questions?"

"Just one - how about a threesome sometime?"

The Lawns did not feign their disgust.

* * * * *

Topper Bello's suicide was reported on various front pages and local TV news. He had been a well-known character, usually good for a pithy quote, and a regular patron of many bartenders. A half-hearted search for a reason for his plunge led nowhere. Roy Incisor spoke at the memorial service - carefully avoiding even a hint of what he knew about the scandal surrounding the late Demo chairman.

B.O. Nicely left that same service determined to press on. Without his co-conspirator anything might happen and the chairman instinctively settled on the worst. Christ, he had to face it and do it now before there was a leak. He was consumed by it. "It" being how the world was going to learn of the disgusting Gunter S.S. B.O. told himself he was not a Joe McCarthy with a pitiful list of alleged commies. No, this caper was a civic duty and the message must be carried by the people's guardians - the press.

B.O. made it a big deal, "scary and confidential" when he made the calls. "This won't be an exclusive, I'm telling each paper - no TV. This story demands accuracy and fairness, that rules out TV news. Anyway, my office at noon, can I expect you?"

He snared the big three - just what he wanted. The political editors were quite prompt. Rarely did Johnnie Plum of the <u>Call</u>, Ace Movement of the <u>Ex</u>, and Lulu Rombus of the <u>News</u> sit together in the same room. Today they were seated around a table in the GOP chairman's office and B.O. had his speech well rehearsed.

"Thanks for coming. I am so shocked and dismayed about the appalling events surrounding this election. First, my dear friend and worthy opponent, Topper Bello, left us." B.O. paused and wiped his eyes with his pink silk pocket hankie. "Then this - I'm reeling."

"What is 'this', B.O.?" asked Johnnie.

B.O. reached for a large envelope and then threw it on the table. "Pictures...disgusting, filthy pictures. See for yourselves."

And they did.

"Where did these come from?" Lulu was red in the face, shaking and shaken.

B.O., a very serious B.O., replied, "The envelope was shoved under my door, musta been last night. It was here when I got in this morning."

Johnnie Plum had been carefully studying the images since they were pulled from the envelope. He gruffly said, "So are these real? Not doctored are they? Is this Gunther or his double? What do you want us to do, B.O.? Run these pics on the family page?"

"I'm not releasing these horrible pictures to the press or anybody else - yet. I don't want this sicko in Congress that's my message. The public should know and your esteemed papers should tell it. I don't see what else there is for me to do at this time. Somebody must expose the sodomite, but it's not me. This filth is not for distribution."

Lulu asked, "What are you doing here, B.O., if not distributing? We're going to be all over this and I mean big time." She wasn't kidding.

Grey-haired, scabby heads were scratched and not a few clumps of dandruff flew in editors' offices. The story was preposterous but three independent witnesses saw the pictures. It came down to the rival political editors vouching for each other. You don't keep a colossal scandal under wraps. It was the buzz of insiders at all the newspapers. A gossip columnist slipped an item in "…[P]olitics again…this time a well-known candidate has more than bared it all, and there are pictures, too!"

The papers each held the story, looking for confirmation and desperately seeking Gunther. Rumors were epidemic. Pressure finally drove the Democratic candidate under the covers. He went to bed and stayed there silent and sweating. Gunther decided to quit the race and move to Arkansas. His resignation, withdrawal or whatever would be in writing. He wasn't going to let those animals from the press get near him. But what did he know?

Roy had LIVE/DIE at the printers and ready to go. We, too, were on hold waiting for the Lawns to Puke on Duke. They came to my law office unannounced and took over the conference room from our befuddled receptionist.

"Confirmation is a sensation we adore." Boy, I was getting tired of these brats, even if they did deliver.

Once again the Lawns pranced around like show dogs, singing away, each twisting a baton with battery operated lights on each end.

"Yeth, Thonny, we have it all. Identical twins, ethtranged it theems, one a fun loving guy and the other a politician. Tho, fun brother does hith thing in front of camerath - the thordid pictureth are to be uthed againtht the politician brother and who will know? Well, we do."

They exchanged smiles and launched a brief, but complicated twirling technique.

"So, dear Roy has our copy. We thaved Gunther... we predict. The viciousneth and thqualor of the thkeme should make Mr. and Mrth. Voter plenty pithed at the GOP." More smug smiles.

The other one said, "We're off to the Russian River for the weekend. Our *expose* will be on the stands Monday morning - we'll be here to deal with our colleagues from the fourth estate."

I stood up and did the right thing, "Great, I mean sensational. You gents will be receiving accolades and a bonus. LIVE/DIE is going to launch like an astronaut's pecker."

While our ace reporters spent the weekend at leisure, I helped Roy, Dede and Barbara with the phones. Of course, the story, or parts of it, had leaked. My guess was the printing plant or rather somebody who worked there was on the take. The copy itself did not get out...what we had to contend with was all rumor and guesses. It's easy to stonewall at least for a couple of days...and that we did.

Dad called on Saturday to say that he and Anita were headed out of town "to renew our wows." At the moment, his phone was never silent. They fled accordingly.

So with minimal duties on Saturday and Sunday I had Astrid to myself. Or did she have me? The girl professed to like her midnight shift - "It's easier to avoid your attacks." I found it fairly easy to work around that schedule. She cooperated fully and that was the weekend that I realized my lust was also love... real, all-American love. So I proposed.

She said, "Stay tuned."

Whoops, that sent me on a downward spiral. I managed, "I'm not withdrawing my offer - ever."

I had seen the galleys of LIVE/DIE, of course, but on Monday morning when I passed a couple of newsstands I wallowed in pride. The magazine was prominently displayed each place I checked. Under the masthead was a stark white cover. In large red letters were the words, "HOW ROTTEN." That was it... powerful, simple and as Dad said, "Classy."

The afternoon paper was first off the tee. Evening news on the tube had it big and in a couple of cases almost right. The story rolled for days. National press showed as did network news. It was all great fun, especially for the Lawns who sort of played it straight. At least in their comments to publication. But whoever first said, "Boys will be boys," was so, so right. A scandal sheet published a shot of the Lawns each on an arm of Aunt Verda; the trio was walking along the Embarcadero. Juan and John were wearing kid's sailor suits.

The headlines and comments were the reward. Not that the magazine didn't sell out. And we sold tons of ad pages for the future. What caught my eye?

"The Queer Smear…GOP Caught Playing Dirty With Dirt."

"Gunther S.S. Stays in Race…Vows to Hose Down Porno."

"GOP Chairman B.O. Nicely Resigns; To Spend More Time with Family."

"Rommel Brother Says, 'My Movies Cleaner Than Politics.'"

"B.O. Sinc Wants No Part of 'Putrid Party' - Quits Race."

"New LIVE/DIE Mag Big Hit - Publisher Codfish Brac Takes All Credit."

And from the social page, "Dr. Astrid Farley and Atty. Sonny Brac have announced their engagement."

And from a media column, "The dynamo duo, Juan and John Lawn (they put the b.o. on B.O.) are leaving the Bay Area for an assignment in the nation's capitol. 'We have been engaged by the Bureau of Virtue to investigate the sexual proclivities of each and every member of Congress. This should take the rest of our lives.'"